# What if *she*

The idea tantalized.

Sara glanced at Alec from beneath her lashes, shocked to find he was staring at her. She turned to face him, licking her lips in nervousness.

His expression didn't change, but the air became supercharged. Could she do this?

Daringly, she moved closer still, until her mouth brushed his.

His response was instantaneous and all she could have hoped for when he pulled her into his arms and opened his mouth against hers.

**To have and to hold...**

Their marriage was meant to last—
and they have the gold rings to prove it!

**To love and to cherish...**

But what happens when their promise
to love, honor and cherish is put to the test?

**From this day forward...**

Emotions run high as husbands and wives discover
how precious—and fragile—their wedding vows are....
Will true love keep them together—forever?

**Marriages meant to last!**

Look out in October for
*His Trophy Wife* (#3672)
by Leigh Michaels

Barbara loves to hear from readers.
You can contact her at www.barbaramcmahon.com

# THE MARRIAGE TEST
## *Barbara McMahon*

TO HAVE AND TO HOLD

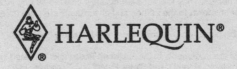

# HARLEQUIN®

TORONTO • NEW YORK • LONDON
AMSTERDAM • PARIS • SYDNEY • HAMBURG
STOCKHOLM • ATHENS • TOKYO • MILAN • MADRID
PRAGUE • WARSAW • BUDAPEST • AUCKLAND

ISBN 0-373-03669-8

THE MARRIAGE TEST

First North American Publication 2001.

Visit us at www.eHarlequin.com

Printed in U.S.A.

# CHAPTER ONE

ALEC BLACKSTONE stood beside his suitcase watching the Jeep bounce gently down the sloping road. Once around the bend, the sound of the engine faded.

Silence enveloped him.

He gazed around in disgust. Trees. A million trees. The sun shone in a cloudless sky. Through the glossy leaves and long needles, he could see the gleam of sunlight reflecting on the lake a short distance away. The sweet scent of honeysuckle mingled with the pungent scent of pine wafting on the warm springtime air.

Without warning one of the now-familiar dizzy spells struck. He reached out to steady himself with the porch railing, clunking the heavy cast. That started his arm throbbing again. Biting off an expletive, he waited until the dizziness passed. Nothing like a reality check to remind him why he was in some backwater resort instead of striding into court for a case, or meeting with opposing counsel.

Ignoring the pounding ache in his right arm, he reached for his suitcase and laptop with his left hand and turned to enter the log cabin. That accident must have addled his brains. What was he doing here, sequestered in some hideaway retreat when Boston was his normal turf?

While appearing rustic, the cottage purported to

provide all the conveniences a guest could wish. Or so Wyatt had told him.

Alec wished Wyatt and Elizabeth had never suggested he take their spot at the resort. Or that he hadn't been foolish enough to agree. He could have managed fine at his apartment. He wasn't going to recuperate any faster in some out-of-the-way resort in the Adirondack Mountains of upstate New York. However long it took to heal was however long it would take.

Nothing for it now. He was here and would make the most of it—as long as he had his cell phone to keep in touch with the office. He'd brought his portable computer, too. He could hook up the modem and have his secretary forward anything he needed to deal with. If he had to print something, surely he could get a ride into a decent size town to find a printer? His secretary could always mail anything that wasn't urgent.

Stepping inside, Alec noticed without much curiosity how spacious the living room was—with its high ceiling and huge old stone fireplace. Even though it was May, it got cool in the evenings in the mountains. He'd enjoy a fire to take the chill off at night.

Open stairs along one wall led to the second floor. Tucked almost under them in the rear was a swinging door—probably leading to the kitchen. But there was time enough to explore. What else did he have to do for the next three weeks?

Placing his laptop computer on a small table near the door, Alec carried his bag upstairs. There were two doors, both opened, and through each he saw a bed, a dresser and a table. It didn't matter which bedroom he chose. He turned left.

The room was long with a sloping ceiling—elevated in the center yet barely high enough to avoid hitting his head at the side wall. Something to be avoided at all costs after receiving that concussion.

Unpacking didn't take long. He glanced around when he finished, checked his watch, frowning. It wasn't even noon. What was he supposed to do for the rest of the day?

He'd packed a few bestsellers, but didn't feel like reading.

With his headaches and the dizziness that hit unexpectedly, he didn't dare wander far from the cabin.

Great, he was stuck in the back of beyond with nothing to do and eighteen long days ahead of him. He'd never make it without going stark-raving crazy!

A door slammed.

Had he left the front door ajar and the wind blown it shut? No, he was certain he'd closed it. Slowly descending the stairs, he heard a noise from the back of the house. Had the resort personnel brought food? He hadn't even thought about that yet and suddenly realized that as isolated as he was, without a car, meals could prove a problem.

Naturally he could call the front desk and have them send a Jeep to take him to the main lodge. The restaurant there was supposed to be four stars. He didn't have to cook if he didn't want to. Yet, as often as he ate out, he might like the novelty of cooking for himself. Once he felt better.

Pushing open the swinging door to the kitchen, Alec stopped in total surprise. A woman casually dressed in jeans and a long checked shirt leaned against the counter, obviously waiting for the tea-kettle to boil.

A very familiar woman.

But someone he had never expected to see here! And while the face was familiar, the body sure wasn't.

He felt the shock like a kick in the gut, his eyes unable to leave her waist. *Sara was pregnant?*

"What the hell is going on?" he roared. Shock blocked out any delight he might have felt at seeing her. Known for his ability to analyze new testimony instantly, his mind inexplicably shut down. He could only stare dumbfounded at her trying to absorb what he was seeing.

The world seemed to tilt on its axis.

"Alec?" She spun around. Her black hair gleamed in the sunlight streaming in through the tall windows. While almost as short as his at the back, she grew it longer on the sides where it covered the tips of her ears. The feathery bangs normally made her dark eyes look large and mysterious. Now they held shocked disbelief.

His gaze was still locked at her waist as he tried to take in the fact that his wife, whom he hadn't seen in months, was pregnant. Very pregnant. And he hadn't known a thing about it!

"What are you doing here?" Sara asked.

"Never mind me." He looked up at her and caught the wary look in her face. "Was there something you needed to tell me?'' he asked softly, his voice as hard as tempered steel.

He watched as she swallowed, her gaze never leaving his. Taking a breath she stalled for time as a myriad of expressions crossed her face.

''I'm pregnant,'' she said at last.

Fury burned as he continued to stare, the strength of his feelings foreign to him. Normally he could control his emotions, but not in the face of this.

''Who's the father?'' he asked.

She reacted as if he'd slapped her, her head snapping back, her eyes widening.

''You are, of course!'' she retorted, color flooding her cheeks. ''What a rotten thing to say. Whose else could it be?''

''I have no idea. You walked out on me, remember?''

He didn't have a lot of experience with pregnant women, but she looked enormous. ''How far along are you?''

She hesitated only a moment before replying. ''Almost eight months.''

''Eight months! In all that time you couldn't pick up the phone to call and let me know about this?'' Anger grew. If she was truly pregnant with his child, why hadn't she let him know? No matter how far apart they'd grown, there was no excuse to keep this from him! Her leaving had left a hole in his life. To compound the situation by deliberately keeping him in the dark about their baby was inexcusable.

''Or maybe there's another reason,'' he said silkily, wanting to hear her denial again, afraid she might not repeat it.

She tilted her chin up and glared at him. "I resent your implications. I didn't leave you to go to some other man. You know full well why I left."

"I know why you *said* you were leaving. Did being pregnant have anything to do with it?"

"Of course not. I didn't know I was pregnant when I left."

He eyed her considerable girth, lifting one eyebrow in skepticism. "I shouldn't think it could have been long afterward that you found out."

She shrugged, crossing her arms over her chest as if in protection.

"I should have told you, I guess," she said reluctantly.

"You guess!"

"All right, it was wrong. I kept meaning to..."

He waited. Years of dealing with criminals had honed his technique. Most people were uncomfortable with extended silence and would rush to fill the void.

"I—the time was just never right," she said.

"Did you *ever* plan to tell me?" he asked, trying to hold on to the emotions that threatened to overwhelm him. How dare she keep this from him! No matter how their marriage had ended, she should have told him as soon as she discovered she was pregnant! It was *his* baby, too.

"Yes, of course."

"When? After he graduated from college?"

"I don't know. When the time was right."

"Do Wyatt and Elizabeth know?"

She nodded.

Dammit! Alec wanted to smash something. His own brother had known and not told him. His fist hit the doorjamb in frustration.

Sara crossed to the table, turned and paced back, as if she couldn't stay still. "You could have called," she said at last.

"*You* left *me*. You knew where I was."

"And if you had cared at all, you would have called at least once to see if I was all right."

He narrowed his eyes. "Are you all right? Is the pregnancy normal?"

"I'm fine, that's not the point."

"And the point is?"

"That if you didn't care enough about me to see if I was doing all right why would I think you would be interested in learning you were about to become a father?"

*A father.* He wasn't ready. The only time they'd talked about children, he'd insisted they wait. He wasn't sure he would ever be ready to assume that role in someone's life. Moot point now. It looked as if the choice had been taken from him—which instantly sparked another thought. Had she deliberately gotten pregnant?

Sara narrowed her eyes. "So what are you doing here?"

"I'm staying here. Did you do this on purpose?"

"What, come here? And you can't *stay. I'm* staying here!"

"I meant, did you deliberately get pregnant?"

She shook her head vehemently. "I guess no birth control is foolproof. You have to admit the timing is terrible—a single woman, no husband in the picture."

"Because of *your* departure."

She shrugged. "We could argue the point all night. But you need to find other accommodation."

"Wyatt and Elizabeth booked this place for their vacation. When he got that assignment in Europe and decided to leave early to vacation there, he offered me use of this place." Offered was a euphemism. Wyatt had practically forced it down Alec's throat. But Sara didn't need to know that. She had forfeited her right to know anything about him. Wasn't that the way she wanted it?

He frowned, was that the way she felt, too—that he had no right to know about her? Was that why she hadn't told him about the baby?

"Elizabeth offered the place to me. I wanted to get away and this was perfect," Sara said in dismay. "She didn't say anything about your coming here."

"Maybe Wyatt didn't tell her." Or maybe his brother and sister-in-law had plotted what they saw as a perfect setup to get Alec and Sara together to see if they could patch up their marriage.

Only neither knew the full situation. There was no marriage left to patch up.

"Well, I'm sorry, but I've been planning this for a while. You'll have to make other arrangements," Sara said shortly.

"How could you have been planning this for long? They just learned a week ago about the trip to

Europe.'' The day before the car crash that had broken his arm and given him a concussion.

''I've been planning time off from work for months. This was a perfect start to my maternity leave. Elizabeth suggested this place to me last week.''

''If you are close enough to delivery to go on maternity leave, what are you doing out here, miles from the nearest hospital?'' If she didn't have sense enough to take care of herself, she should at least think of the baby.

''I have enough time, there's more than six weeks before the baby's due. I'll be back in Boston in plenty of time to deliver. I checked with my doctor, she said it was all right.''

How many other people had known about the baby? Alec wondered, anger still churning. How could all of them think it was better that the father not know?

Sara appeared nervous, he recognized the signs. Well she should be. He hadn't been this angry when she'd walked out. The knowledge he was about to become a father was overwhelming. She'd had eight months to get used to the idea of becoming a mother—he'd been denied that time.

''Where are you living? Do you need help with the baby?''

''A little late for that, don't you think?''

''And whose fault is that? Dammit, Sara, you should have told me!''

''And what would you have done?'' she challenged, hands on her hips as she glared at him.

Bravado, he suspected. He could tell she was putting up a front. Feeling guilty, maybe, for withholding the news?

"Made sure you were home where you belonged," he said, stepping closer. He could smell the fragrance she always wore, and memories ached. It had been too long. Without thought, he pulled her into his arms and kissed her.

Sensations erupted unexpectedly. The kiss was wild and exciting—and as passionate as ever—despite the anger that bubbled just below the surface. He'd not forgotten a thing about the complex, confusing woman whom he'd married eighteen months ago. For a moment it was like coming home. She tasted the same—sweet as honey. And the explosion of his senses was fantastic—like they'd never been apart, as if the differences that separated were swept away—

Then the awkwardness of their embrace penetrated as he became aware of her protruding stomach. She definitely didn't *feel* like the woman he'd married!

Raising his head, he gazed down into her shimmering eyes. She pulled back and crossed her arms over her chest defensively.

"If you didn't have time for me when we lived together, why would I think you'd make time for a baby?" she asked bluntly.

"That wasn't your decision to make. You should have told me," he said. Spinning around he strode from the room, slapping the swinging door out of the way in an effort to dissipate some of the roiling emotions that still choked him. He didn't stop until he

was on the porch. He saw nothing of the beauty before him, not the trees, the lake nor the cloudless sky.
The only reality in his world was the fact he'd just
learned his wife was almost eight months pregnant.
And he hadn't known.

As the endless moment passed, he considered her
question—what would he have done? Insisted she
move back into their apartment? Learned everything
he could about babies in the months he had until it
arrived? Readjusted his thinking to accept the fact he
was soon to become a father?

God, *he was going to be a father!* He knew nothing about the job!

Sara stood still, watching Alec storm from the room,
her knees feeling as shaky as a wet noodle. She
couldn't think straight. His kiss had been angry, but
it hadn't mattered. For one glorious moment, she'd
been immersed in the delight of his embrace—which
she'd thought she'd never experience again. She certainly had never envisioned a kiss under these cir-
cumstances.

What had gone so wrong between them? And
why?

Turning as the teakettle whistled shrilly, she
switched off the gas and stared at the kettle, unable
to move. Seeing him had been a shock. The feelings
that had initially flared gave way to guilt when he
appeared so stunned at the discovery.

She should have told him months ago. Should
have let him share in the anticipation of the birth of
their baby. Guilt swept through, built. He was right,

she'd been wrong. And she didn't like the feeling. But the time had never seemed right.

She'd wanted to shout with jubilation when she found out—but their marriage had already ended and she'd felt she had enough to cope with.

No, all the excuses in the world wouldn't justify her keeping the news a secret. She took a deep breath. She had to make things right—or as right as she could given the situation.

Slowly she walked from the room. Where was he?

The front door stood open. She could see him standing at the porch railing, staring off across the expanse of clearing, toward the lake. She'd rather go to the dentist than face this, but there was no choice. She didn't know when she'd see him again, best to get it done.

"Alec?" she said pushing open the screen door.

He turned slowly, studied her, giving nothing away in his expression.

"If you didn't know I'd be here, why did you come?"

He held up his cast. "I needed a place to recuperate. Wyatt insisted I use the cabin. They'd already paid the deposit when their plans changed." He shrugged. "It was easier to come than argue with him."

She blinked in surprise. She'd known about the accident, but not how much of a toll it had taken on Alec. He must have been more seriously injured than Wyatt and Elizabeth had let on for him not to argue. Alec liked nothing better than to debate issues—

sometimes taking an unpopular stance for the sheer joy of the discussion.

Her eyes darkened. She hesitated for a long moment, then reluctantly said, "I knew about the accident. Elizabeth assured me you would be all right. That's true, isn't it?"

"So they say," he said succinctly.

"How did it happen? You're such a good driver." She shivered, folding her arms across her chest. "Elizabeth called me immediately. Knowing how you felt about me, I didn't come to the hospital."

He looked surprised, then swayed, reaching out to grasp the porch railing.

"Are you all right?" she asked, taking a step forward.

"I received a concussion in the wreck and still get dizzy spells. According to the doctor, they'll stop one of these days."

"Why don't you sit down? Want a cup of tea?" She reached out to him as if to place her hand on his arm. His look had her dropping her arm and stepping back. Nothing could be clearer—he didn't need her, or want her. Hadn't she learned that when they were together?

Alec walked carefully to the nearest chair.

She hovered nearby, wishing she still had the right to fuss over him. The accident had scared her. Before that she'd never imagined a world without Alec in it—even if they had separated. She wished she could tell him that. But the words didn't come. Just a weary acceptance of the way things had gone, and the fact there was nothing to be done to change the past.

\*   \*   \*

Alec leaned back in the chair and closed his eyes. The dizziness was starting to fade but he didn't want to watch Sara. He shouldn't have reacted so strongly to discovering she was pregnant. And he damn well should not have kissed her!

"I apologize, Alec. I should have told you about the baby as soon as I found out," she said stiffly.

Damn right, she should have. The anger still simmered. He slitted his eyes, seeing her lean against the porch support, gazing sadly out toward the lake. She still moved with a graceful manner despite her pregnancy. He'd always liked watching her. She seemed so very feminine—and desirable.

Not for the first time he began to wonder what his life would have been like had his mother not deserted her family. Or if his father had remarried a loving, giving woman, instead of growing into the bitter, withdrawn man he'd become. Maybe he would have known how to hold on to his wife, how to stay married.

Closing his eyes again, he reminded himself he'd made it thirty-four years without a woman in his life, he could manage the next thirty-four. The months he and Sara had been married didn't count.

Though, he corrected himself, technically, they were still married.

And now had a baby on the way!

"Did you think I'd make a lousy father, is that why you didn't tell me about the baby?" he asked when the silence stretched out.

# CHAPTER TWO

"NO, NOT a lousy father, just an absent one. When would you see the baby?" She shrugged. "I guess I didn't think your knowing would have changed anything—especially your working hours."

He motioned to the chair opposite. "Sit down. We have a situation to deal with."

She sat gingerly on the edge of a chair. "I don't expect anything from you," she said quickly.

"It's my baby, too, right?"

Nodding her head emphatically, Sara looked calmer than he felt.

"Do you need anything?"

She shook her head. "Last month I moved into a two-bedroom apartment, fixed up the second bedroom for the baby. We'll be fine."

He didn't like her answer. But what could he say? She'd made her feelings clear when she'd left.

"And about the cottage..."

She watched him warily. "There might be another cottage available you could use," she offered.

"Or one you could use."

"I'm not moving, I'm all unpacked."

"So am I."

Impasse.

Out of nowhere, Alec raised his left hand to his

forehead shakily and tried to look injured. "I'm recovering from a serious automobile crash."

Sara burst out laughing. "I don't believe it. Surely you're not trying to play on my sympathies?" she asked. "That doesn't sound like you at all."

At least not the man she'd married echoed in the silence.

"Wouldn't work, would it?" He frowned, he couldn't imagine what had led to that pathetic attempt at humor.

"Not a chance. You'll do a lot to get your own way, but I'm not leaving. You'll have to find other accommodation."

The light discussion was a relief after the intensity of his emotions. It would take a while to adjust to the coming change in his life. Seeing her balanced on the edge of the chair reminded him how he'd missed her when she first left. How empty the apartment had seemed. How long the nights.

"I'm sure there is some legal precedence for my staying," he said slowly, feeling the anger gradually dissipate. He had a lot to think about, but first, he wanted to get their lodging settled.

"If there were, I'm sure you'd find it. We could draw straws," she suggested, ignoring his feeble attempt to bluff.

"Or I could just stay."

"*I'm* staying," she retorted firmly. She hadn't moved, but for some reason Alec felt as if she were digging in for a long campaign. He knew she could be tenacious and stubborn. Hadn't he seen her going toe to toe with the senior members of her firm when she felt strongly about something? And seen her win!

And hadn't she walked out just as she'd threatened when he hadn't changed his lifestyle to suit her?

For a long moment they stared at each other. But Alec wasn't a top-notch assistant district attorney for nothing. He had years of experience in negotiation, in cutting deals with criminals to appear to cooperate while getting them—and others of their like—off the streets. He'd call her bluff.

"All right, we both stay."

Sara blinked. "Both?" It was almost a squeak.

"I could say, all three. Or you can leave." The gauntlet was thrown. Alec was curious to find out what she would do now.

Leaning back in her chair, Sara stared at the man. Was he out of his mind? A husband and wife who had separated didn't share a house together! Sara had come to the resort to spend time alone, to come to terms with the way her life was going. Make plans for the future. Consider asking for a divorce. She didn't want to have Alec around while she made that tough decision.

She had never been able to ignore him. There was too much energy around the man, too much sex appeal. Taller than her own five feet ten, he easily measured six feet four. With his dark hair and dark eyes, they could almost be confused for brother and sister. Though the look in his eyes never made her feel at all sisterly.

She frowned and dropped her gaze. She had no business feeling anything. Their marriage had ended six months ago. She was doing fine on her own. And soon she'd have her precious baby. She had to get things settled in her life so she'd be ready to focus on her baby when he or she arrived.

The last thing she wanted was an emotional entanglement at this stage.

"I was planning to stay the three weeks Wyatt and Elizabeth booked," she said slowly. Maybe he'd stay a day or two and grow bored—that was too long a time for him to stay away from work. For a moment the old bitterness rose. Work would soon claim his total attention—she knew that firsthand.

"I'm under strict orders to stay away from work for three full weeks," he said wryly.

She looked up at that, meeting his gaze again. The fluttering in her heart surprised her. "Whose orders?" She couldn't imagine Alec taking orders from anyone. He was too self-assured, self-confident. Sometimes she had even thought him too arrogant. She'd loved teasing him about that. The memory hurt.

"My doctor," he replied.

"Oh. To recover fully from the accident?"

He looked away, his expression impassive. "Among other things. So do we agree to stay, or fight it out now?"

She looked away sadly. That's what they'd come to? Fighting? She remembered their whirlwind courtship. She'd felt so cherished, so desired.

"I suppose we could share the place. I mean, if we were staying in the main lodge, we might have ended up with adjacent rooms. So this wouldn't be much different." Even as she said the words, she scrambled around for another idea. Only nothing came to mind. Could they really share?

She felt at a loss. If they agreed to share a cabin, what else would he expect? To spend time together? Share their vacation? She had been looking forward to the solitude. And how could she decide whether to take that next step in severing their marriage ties with her own emotions muddled by Alec's presence?

He still had the ability to start her heart racing and she didn't know how she was going to keep a cool head if faced with him every day.

Would he try to kiss her again? Heat flared through her at the memory of that kiss. She couldn't allow that, it would truly muddy the waters.

"Do we have a deal?"

"I guess."

Should she bring up the kiss? No, that would attach more importance than it deserved. If staying got to be too much, she could always cut short her trip and return home. Maybe it wouldn't be so bad with them both on neutral territory, so to speak.

"Fine. I have to call the office. I'll see you later."

She watched as he rose and entered through the front door. Had she thought being here would make a difference? Nothing had changed. She should be amazed he'd lasted this long without being in touch with his precious office. Obviously his doctor's orders to rest only meant a change of venue, not complete abstinence from work!

A few moments later she heard the murmur of his voice. He'd obviously brought his own phone. The resort didn't have outside lines from the cottages. The whole purpose of coming was to escape the normal routines of life. To relax and recharge.

But not for Alec. He still had that restless energy, that same inability to stay away from work. It had been that obsession that had ended their marriage. And made her wary about trusting her heart to another man ever again.

His inability to reach a balance between their marriage and work had been the cause of her leaving. Even now, she searched for ways she could have changed things. No solution had ever appeared. The cold, hard, unpalatable fact was Alec preferred fighting with the criminal element to spending time with his wife.

And learning they were having a baby obviously hadn't changed that.

A half hour later, after having her cup of tea, Sara wandered down the worn path through the trees to the lake. There were wooden docks jetting into the water along the shore with rowboats and tandem paddle wheels tied up to each. Several boats dotted the expanse of the lake as other vacationers took advantage of their availability.

She had met the guests in the two neighboring cottages yesterday afternoon. Spotting James and Hilary battling one of the paddle wheel boats, she waved. They grinned and waved back, obviously delighting in their attempts to control the direction of the unwieldy craft using only the bicycle pedals.

Sara watched and laughed. They were so young, so happy, so in love—but then, honeymooners were always cheerful. For a moment the smile faded. She had had such high hopes for her own marriage. They'd been eroded during the months she and Alec had lived together. How different their marriage had turned out. She'd expected more—more than Alec could deliver anyway. Now all she had was a few happy memories, and a truckload of regrets.

Suddenly feeling very old at twenty-eight, Sara turned and ambled along the shore. It was peaceful here. She ought to be able to regain her sense of self, make plans for the future. Make the hard decisions that faced her.

"Hello young lady," Mrs. Simpson greeted her. The elderly woman and her husband smiled at Sara from their seat on a fallen log near the beach. In the shade, it was protected from the sun, while offering a perfect view of the lake.

"Hi, lovely day, isn't it?" Sara stopped to visit with the neighbors on the far side of her cabin, the Simpsons. The opposite end of the spectrum from the honeymooners, she thought whimsically. Married more than fifty years, they still retained a glow of love.

Which only served to prove it could be done.

Sara chatted with them for a few minutes, then moved on. Long, happy marriages could be achieved. She wondered what the secret was, and why she apparently lacked whatever it took.

Sara had not known how to deal with Alec's tendencies to put work before all else. She never remembered her father doing that, before he'd died when she'd been young. It was obvious in retrospect that arguing and pleading had been the wrong approach. But would anything have changed the outcome?

Returning home after a nice ramble, she pushed open the door to the living room, moving quietly in case he was still on the phone. Alec lay on the sofa—fast asleep. His cell phone had dropped on the floor beside him.

She tiptoed over and studied him, aware of his powerful masculine appeal even in sleep. She had loved waking up first when they'd lived together savoring that quiet time when she could watch him sleep. The warmth of the memories filled her—and she smiled sadly, remembering all those times she'd had him solely to herself. There'd been no work to interfere, no prior commitments. Just the two of them in their own world.

Which usually ended as soon as he awoke each day.

Picking up the phone, she checked to make sure it was not still connected. Laying it quietly on the coffee table, she headed for the kitchen.

As she nibbled a sandwich for lunch, she speculated about his accident. Elizabeth hadn't said what caused it and once the initial panic had eased, Sara hadn't pursued it. She'd been shocked how strong her own reactions at hearing the news had been. Once she knew he was going to be all right, she'd deliberately distanced herself. She had to protect herself, and getting involved with Alec again was not an option!

Still, she was curious. Had the crash involved a

drunk driver? Had anyone else been hurt? Was he truly going to be completely fit again soon?

Would he forgive her for not telling him about the baby?

The cell phone rang. She jumped up and ran to get it. Before she could reach it, however, Alec woke and snagged it from the table. Slowly he sat up, speaking, then listening.

He met Sara's eyes, and gave a half wave, his attention immediately caught by the caller.

Some things never changed, she thought wryly as she climbed the stairs for an afternoon nap, one of the luxuries of vacationing.

She suspected his doctor had not intended for Alec to continue work, she thought as she slipped off her shoes and lay down on the comfortable bed. In fact, he would be better off at the office than trying to do everything from a remote cabin.

As she drifted to sleep, she could hear the murmur of Alec's voice. What could be so important he couldn't take a few days to relax and recuperate?

It would never work, Alec thought late in the afternoon. He'd searched every inch of the cabin, except for Sara's bedroom, and not found a single phone jack. There was a direct line to the main lodge, but they couldn't patch him through to an outside line.

Didn't the resort management know people needed to keep in touch with the rest of the world? If he hadn't brought his cell phone, he would be totally cut off! He needed to get his computer hooked up somewhere to receive the fax his secretary wanted to send.

Pacing the living room, he examined each wall again, hoping he'd just missed seeing a jack. He didn't need this frustration on top of the news he'd discovered that morning. For a moment he wondered when he'd feel in control again. Or would having a baby disrupt his life so totally he'd never get it back on track?

"It's really pretty outside and warm. No need to do all your exercise inside," Sara said.

He spun around. She'd paused halfway down the stairs to watch him.

"I was looking for a phone jack for an outside line, not taking a walk," he snapped, his frustration bubbling over. This frustration was not all work related. How was he supposed to share a cabin with her and ignore the attraction that still flared whenever he saw her? To ignore the anger that he couldn't dislodge at not being told his wife was pregnant.

"There aren't any. I think there is a guest office you can use in the conference center at the main lodge, but none of the cabins are wired for phones. The purpose for coming here is to relax, not change the location of work. Where did you think you were coming?"

"To the back of beyond, but I at least thought I could communicate with the rest of the world." He ran his left hand through his hair. He didn't have time for this! Not the inconvenience nor the feelings that stirred when Sara came into the room.

He'd gotten over her. She'd made her position

clear. He wanted to move on, not be reminded of what they'd once had.

He'd have to call for a Jeep to pick him up and take him to the main lodge. How long would that take? Glancing at his watch, he saw it was getting late.

She continued down the steps, watching him warily.

"I guess you came here for a different reason than what Wyatt and Elizabeth suggested."

"I wouldn't be here at all if it wasn't for the blasted wreck. Cutting back and resting up is one thing, being cut off is another. And as far as I know, Wyatt and Elizabeth were coming on some sort of second honeymoon. Why, I can't imagine. They've only been married two years."

Sara smiled.

He paused and stared at her, frowning. "What?"

"You truly can't imagine why they'd want a second honeymoon?"

The amusement in her eyes sidetracked him, entranced him. He shook his head. He had work to do! There were cases coming to court soon. He had to make sure they had all the facts nailed down to get a conviction. And the new law clerk needed direction. There was too much to do to be spinning fantasies about his wife again.

Once had been a hard-learned lesson. And the result enough of a disaster to make sure he never again ventured down that path!

"Face it, Alec. Wyatt and Elizabeth love each other. They want to spend time together just the two of them. It's what most husbands and wives do—to take time to talk about what's important to them, build memories, make a family.''

''Most husbands and wives plan a family together,'' he said, frowning at her.

The impact continued to hit him—they had made a family, albeit unknowingly!

He knew nothing about being a father. His own hadn't precisely been a stellar example. He had never really planned to take that step but now it was imminent.

''You're nearly eight months pregnant so when exactly is it due?''

''June 21. But it might come later, first babies often do.''

The look of sadness on her face intrigued him. Was she regretting the sudden, abrupt end to their marriage? Regretting the fact she was pregnant?

Alec suddenly felt an urgent need to do something to erase that look from her face, but he hadn't a clue as to what. Sara had always baffled him.

''Do you regret being pregnant?''

She looked startled. ''Not at all. I'm thrilled to be having a baby. My mother is excited to become a grandmother, Wyatt and Elizabeth can't wait—'' She stopped, looked away guiltily.

''So everyone is rejoicing. Except me.''

''You regret it, then?''

He shook his head. ''I'm still reeling under the shock. I haven't had eight months to get used to the idea.''

''I'm sorry. I would undo the past if I could.''

The silence stretched out between them. For a moment he regretted the loss of the adoration Sara had held for him. He'd always felt ten feet tall when she'd turn her eyes to him and simply light up from the inside.

"Come with me to the main lodge. You can look around the gift shop or something while I wait for my fax," he suggested impulsively, suddenly wishing to see that guilty look disappear from her face.

Didn't all women like to shop? Not that he remembered Sara doing much of that when they were married. Except when she dragged him out to look at furniture. That had been a fun day. She'd made it an afternoon full of laughter and nonsense. He'd forgotten about it until now. He guessed he owed her some laughter and good memories.

Sara looked at him, tilting her head to one side. It exposed her neck and Alec's gaze was drawn to the slender column. He wanted to brush his fingertips along its length to see if her skin was still as soft and warm as he remembered. Trace the column with his lips, feel that pulse point at the base of her throat with his tongue. Slide his hands through that short, glossy black hair to see if it still felt silky to touch.

Looking away, he suddenly suspected the car crash had done permanent brain damage. He hadn't felt like this about anyone since he'd been a teenager with raging hormones! He had his work, a select group of friends. The last thing he needed was to get entangled in any kind of relationship. They'd tried it once, and it hadn't worked. Nothing had changed.

The kiss earlier had been a mistake. He'd see it wasn't repeated.

"Okay, I'll go along for the ride, thank you," she said primly.

Turning swiftly, he headed to the wall phone that connected them to the resort lobby. The sooner he got back on track the better! The past was dead. Let it lie, he ordered himself silently.

Picking up his laptop a minute later, he nodded toward the door. "We can wait outside."

Sara shrugged. "I imagine you don't want to waste a single minute. Are you planning to jump into the Jeep as it flies past, or can the driver stop?"

"If he's fast enough, he can stop for us. I need my secretary to fax me a brief before she leaves for the day."

The afternoon was still and warm. Alec stood on the top step, listening for the Jeep. Sara sat down in one of the comfortable chairs as if she was settling in forever.

"Tell me, Alec, did you get hit by a drunk driver?" she asked.

He half turned, to see her and still be able to keep an eye on the road.

"No. I fell asleep at the wheel."

"I always thought work would kill you. It looks as if it almost did."

# CHAPTER THREE

SARA impatiently checked the wall clock over the registration desk for the third time. Alec had said he'd meet her fifteen minutes ago. Where was he?

Dumb question—he was obviously still caught up with whatever fascinating things his secretary was faxing. Sighing gently, she headed down the corridor to the conference wing of the main lodge. Why had she agreed to this stupid trip just to set herself up for more disappointments?

She hesitated outside the glass door. Alec was using one of the desks, his phone caught between his shoulder and his ear, his gaze fixed on his computer screen.

"Disgusting, isn't it."

Sara turned. Another woman stood beside her, glaring at one of the other occupants of the guest services office.

"Disgusting?" Sara asked.

"We came here for a vacation—and he spends his time on the damn phone to the office. I might as well have come by myself." The woman glanced at Sara.

"Same with you?"

Sara shrugged, she had no intention of going into detail about her relationship with Alec. The woman obviously thought they were in the same situation. "Is it a genetic thing with men, do you think?"

The woman laughed. "I'm Molly Harper. The gray-haired man at the desk on the right is my husband, Bill. We haven't had a vacation together in three years and the last one was a combination business trip to Chicago. I loved the place. I doubt Bill remembers anything but the airport. Maybe it is genetic. I'll have to look into his DNA. In the meantime, I plan to salvage at least the rest of the day!"

She pushed open the door and marched over to the desk.

Sara watched, amused. It was easier to feel that emotion when it wasn't her husband. Slowly she shifted her gaze to Alec. What would he do if she marched in to salvage the rest of the day? Probably fall off his chair in shock. Then argue with her as he'd done before.

A moot point. She had no intention of ever again becoming enamored with Alec Blackstone.

Sara watched as Alec frowned at the couple at the next desk. Clicking off his phone, he closed his laptop and stood. The argument grew louder. Looking up, he spotted Sara through the glass wall.

In only a few seconds he'd pushed through the glass door.

"Did you get everything done?" she asked as they turned to head for the lobby.

"Everything was sent. I can read it at the cabin."

"Success!" Molly called as she and her husband came into the hallway. "Good luck with yours."

Sara smiled at her over her shoulder and waved.

"What was that about?" Alec asked.

"They're here on vacation and she's a bit miffed

he's spending time on work. If you're ready, I'm getting hungry. You'd said we'd be leaving a while ago. Next time, if there ever is a next time, I'm bringing a snack!''

He glanced at his watch and nodded.

As they waited for an available Jeep to drive them back to the cabin, Alec asked, "What did that woman mean, good luck with yours?"

"She thought you were my husband and working away your vacation time."

He was silent for a long moment, his eyes searching hers as if looking for something he couldn't find. "And what did you tell her?"

She shrugged. "We didn't exactly stop to chat. She mentioned it in passing before storming into the room to get her husband. I guess she was tired of being ignored."

"Ignored?"

"What do you call it when her husband brings her here and then leaves her for business? I'm fed up with men who can't relate to needs of others. Men who are so self-centered and selfish that only their own desires count. Men who ignore their wives to the detriment of everything they once thought to build. Why marry in the first place, just to get a cook and housekeeper?" Her temper erupted as all the old hurts and insecurities rose.

"Whoa, time out! What touched your hot button? I never married you just to get a cook and housekeeper."

She glared at him. "And why did you marry me? Why sweep me off my feet if I was only to become an encumbrance, something to be shunted aside while you spent your days, and nights, slogging away at work?''

A Jeep pulled to a screeching halt in front of them before Alec could respond. Sara stepped in the back, looking out the far side feeling appalled. She *never* let her temper erupt. What was wrong with her? And what was so wrong about a man doing his best in his job?

''You're going to have a lonely old age,'' she muttered as Alec settled beside the driver.

He turned his head. ''Did you say something?''

She shook her head. She was not out to save the man, just bring some order and focus to her own corner of the world.

When the driver dropped them at the cabin, Sara exited the Jeep on her own. She was hungry and it would take a little while to prepare a meal, but the preparation always soothed her. And she needed soothing after this.

Alec stopped her with a hand on her shoulder. ''Wait a minute, I want to talk with you.''

Startled, she stepped back, almost losing her balance on the three steps leading up to the wide porch. His touch sent tingling sparks skidding across her skin. For a moment, she couldn't think, could only feel. Feel sensations she had thought vanished forever.

''About what?'' Sidestepping away, she faced him from the distance of a few feet. Her breathing felt erratic. Her heart raced.

''You tell me. If we are going to share this place

for a few weeks, we need to set some ground rules.
I don't want you exploding like that if I can avoid
it.''

She tried to organize her thoughts. Some men were
driven to push themselves beyond what they could
handle. Alec had been consumed with work. He had
spent long hours every day at the office, brought
work home at night. If he didn't go in on the week-
ends, it was because he already had stacks of papers
to read at home. Their honeymoon had lasted a week,
and as their marriage progressed, he spent less and
less time with her and more and more at work.

She looked at him, trying to ignore the feelings
that fluttered inside. Trying to ignore the growing
attraction that being with him seemed to engender.
She refused to ever get involved with him again—
even on a casual basis.

But, darn it, her emotions didn't feel casual around
him. Involuntarily her gaze dropped to his lips, remembering again the passion in that kiss. Would he
wish to do it again, without the anger?

Did she want him to?

She stepped back, trying to distance herself from
her own wayward thoughts.

She had learned her lesson and learned it well, she
reminded herself.

''You're here to recuperate, so you said,'' Sara
began.

He nodded.

''Is that all?''

He started to nod his head again, then hesitated.
''Not exactly. According to my doctor, I need to cut

back. To get more rest.'' He moved impatiently, as if he didn't like revealing that fact.

James and Hilary strolled into view, smiling and waving. Sara returned the greeting, her smile feeling forced.

"Who are they?" Alec asked.

"The Martins. They're staying in the next cabin. They're on their honeymoon."

"Do they know we're married?"

Her eyes widened. "I don't know. I hadn't thought about it. I introduced myself yesterday." For a moment Sara tried to remember what they'd discussed. It had been a friendly, casual conversation. She'd said she was on vacation, they'd talked about being married three days and some hours.

She remembered more feeling jaded and cynical in the face of their obviously new love than she could remember the exact words spoken.

"I doubt it came up. They are so in love they only see each other."

"I don't have time for such foolishness," Alec said.

"Meaning marriage?"

"Exactly."

"Neither do I. Once burned, twice shy," Sara said. It obviously worked for others, but not her.

"Then we agree on one thing."

"Absolutely. If they are harboring any delusions we are a happy couple, I'll make sure they understand you are practically a stranger who crashed my vacation and are sharing the house with me because you stubbornly won't go elsewhere. Maybe you should try for a room in the lodge now that you know you'll have to go there to get a phone line for your computer. We wouldn't want to slow down your ability to get more work done each day!''

Alec's gaze narrowed. Was her temper going to flare again? He almost wished it would. Her eyes sparkled, color flew in her cheeks. And the passion that emanated from her when she'd practically yelled while waiting for their ride had been startling, and very interesting.

She'd been cool and distant when telling him she was leaving all those months ago. Now, he was seeing a side he didn't recognize, except in bed. She'd never held back there. For a moment he almost groaned. He couldn't want her—not now. Not after what she'd done.

Yet, his body didn't seem to recognize the restrictions. He wanted to capture that passion, feel the heat of her against him, pour his own pent-up need into her and recapture the ecstasy they'd always found together. That, at least, had never changed.

''I'll work out a schedule, plan to visit the lodge at a certain time each day,'' he said, hoping she didn't recognize any signs of arousal. He'd focus on his anger, and his need to work. Get Sara out of his system once and for all.

She shook her head and stomped by him, opening the door to the cabin. ''Do whatever you want, you will anyway!''

Before she could slam the door behind her, Alec followed her, catching it with his shoulder. He had enough data sent from work to keep him busy until morning. But something wouldn't let him give this up.

"What is it that bothers you so much about my working?" he asked, following her into the kitchen. "I am trying to build a reputation, to get ahead. I'd think a wife would want to support a husband's efforts toward that end."

"I'll tell you." She spun around. "You were already a success when we met. I don't see how poring over reports at all hours of the day or night and talking for hours to cops and other attorneys gets you ahead. You don't know when to cut back. You'll push yourself until you end up killing yourself. That's what you almost did, right? Too tired to stay awake to drive home? No wonder your doctor ordered rest. But you are too consumed to stop. Too arrogant to listen to him. Too stubborn to slow down when you were lucky enough to get a second chance."

"Do you resent me for that?"

"Yes, for all the time I wanted to be with my husband and he wasn't there. For all the nights I wanted someone to talk to, to love, and you weren't there. And I resent the fact you've put me in the position of having to ask for a divorce!" With that, Sara burst into tears.

Nonplussed, Alec stared at her. In all the time he'd known her, he'd never seen her cry. For a moment he almost panicked. He didn't know how to handle a woman in tears. The people he usually dealt with were far beyond the concept of tears. Lowering his laptop to the floor, he took a step forward.

Sara buried her face in her hands, but he heard her sobs, saw her whole body shake with the force of the tears.

Awkwardly, feeling as unsure of himself as a young boy, he encircled her shoulders, trying to keep from whacking her with his cast. He pulled her into his embrace and felt her sag against him, her body shaking, tears soon dampening his shoulder.

"Don't cry."

He wasn't sure she'd heard him. Nothing changed. Could he order her to stop crying? Somehow he felt that wouldn't do any good. He wished Wyatt was here. Maybe he'd know, though maybe not. Elizabeth seemed sublimely happy with his brother. Maybe she never cried.

Teresa, his secretary, would probably know what to do. Didn't she have three daughters?

"Don't cry, Sara," he said again, feeling totally helpless. "I didn't mean to make you cry." At one time he'd only wanted to give her the moon. Give her everything she could ever desire so she wouldn't leave as his mother had.

But he'd blown it. Now there was nothing she wanted from him. And, like his mother, she'd left.

Her hand crept against his shirt, bunching it. The tears continued.

He leaned his head closer. The sweet fragrance he'd smelled earlier enveloped him. He liked it, liked the memories that it brought. Hesitantly he reached up to pat her back, letting his hand move to her head, savoring the silky texture of her hair again. It was still as soft as it looked. What always surprised him was how warm it felt.

"I'm so mad at you," she wailed.

"Why?"

She pushed against his shoulder, stepping back when he released her. Turning, she pulled a paper towel from the roll and blew her nose. Keeping her back to him, she wiped her eyes.

She shrugged. "You are risking your very life for a dumb job. That's such a waste!"

"Sometimes a man has to work to get ahead—"

She spun around and glared at him. Alec noticed the spiky lashes, still drenched in tears. For a moment he remembered he'd heard once that pregnancy lent a certain glow to women. It must be true. Sara looked beautiful—tears, enormous shape and all.

"No! I won't accept that excuse. What are you getting ahead for?"

He didn't want to be discussing this with Sara. He tried to avoid entanglements for this very reason. He felt totally out of his depth, and didn't like it a bit. Give him a clear-cut criminal case, and he was a pro. Not some emotional quagmire that he hadn't a clue how to navigate.

"I wanted to provide you with nice things," he said slowly.

"You're talking about buying *things*. I didn't want *things*. I earn a sufficient salary on my own to enable me to afford a nice apartment, pretty clothes, baby toys. I wanted attention from my husband. You're devoted to work and that's that. Of course, did you ever think about the fact you don't have any outside activities? No hobbies? And you will be all alone in your old age, unless you count Wyatt and Elizabeth. But I don't have to worry about that do I? Nor will you if you keep crashing cars!''

"I work hard because I like it." Why was he defending himself? Was it because he'd heard virtually the same lecture from Wyatt just a week ago?

"And what else do you like?" she challenged.

Alec stared at her. The question echoed and re-echoed. What else did he like? What had he taken time to enjoy over the years? When was the last time he'd gone swimming, or played baseball? What was the last movie he'd seen for the sheer fun of it?

He remembered, and the memory was poignant. They'd gone together, and ended up fighting.

She gave a sad smile. "Go on and get back to your work. It's what defines you." She spun around and pulled out a pot, banging it on the stove.

He cleared his throat. "Shall I plan to eat here?"

"Whatever."

He didn't want to leave. Yet Sara had obviously dismissed him. She was already pulling food from the refrigerator, then a huge frying pan from the lower cupboard.

Feeling disoriented, Alec grabbed his laptop and returned to the living room. He had several papers he had downloaded. His secretary was sending him two briefs and the report she'd drafted for his boss by courier. He'd have them in the morning.

But for the first time in years, the exhilaration of work waned. He placed the computer on the table, walked to the door. Pushing open the screen door, he stepped out on the porch. Sitting on one of the dark green Adirondack chairs, he gazed out across the ground to the glimpse of the lake.

One small mishap and everybody and his brother thought they had the right to chastise him for his chosen way of life. First his doctor, then Wyatt, now Sara. Or Sara again.

Could there be a hint of truth in what they said?

Sara banged the frying pan on the stove, amazed at herself. It was none of her business how Alec Blackstone lived his life. She'd severed the right to care when she'd packed her bags and left.

Shivering, she brushed her hand over the back of her hair, almost feeling Alec's touch. It was the first time she'd cried since leaving. And Alec had been kind.

That was the only reason she was still thinking about him. Not because of the feeling of being safe she'd experienced in his arms. Not for the rippling excitement that danced across her skin when he was near.

And not for the honest bewilderment he'd shown when she started crying. He truly could not understand her position.

She almost laughed. Great, from tears to laughter. Being pregnant certainly disrupted hormones!

As if on cue, the baby moved. Kicking or rolling over, Sara wasn't sure which. She stopped and put her hands on her stomach. A surge of love and devotion centered on the precious life she carried. She'd wanted to start a family almost from the first.

Yet she had held off talking about it with Alec—always waiting for the right time. Odd how things worked out, she thought, wondering if he would ever be happy about it.

If she'd known she was pregnant before she left, would she still have taken that step? Or would she have stayed and continued to try to change things?

Futile thinking.

As the meat browned, she tried to imagine the coming event, but her mind returned to Alec. His body had felt hard and fit. His arms, even with the cast, had held her as if to shelter her from the dangers of the world. For a moment they seemed to connect. Or was it only wishful thinking?

The next week dragged slowly by. Sara stayed as far from Alec as she could. Which wasn't hard as he seemed to be avoiding her at all costs. Sharing the place hadn't proved a hardship after all—unless one counted feeling like she was balancing on a rim, of never feeling comfortable or content, one false step—disaster.

She resented his causing those kind of feelings. She was supposed to be relaxing, instead she felt constantly on edge.

Mealtime was the worst. She quietly prepared her own meals, but it seemed Alec often heard her. He'd step inside the kitchen and lean against the counter, watching her until she'd finally offered to add enough for two.

Twice he went to the lodge to connect with his secretary and stayed to eat dinner there.

Tonight, he'd come in as she began to cook stir-fry, and hung around until she asked if he wanted some. They ate on the porch, enjoying the coolness as the temperature dropped.

"With no television, what do you do in the evenings?" he asked. She already knew he had enough reports and briefs to read he'd never run out of things to do.

"I like to sit by the lake. I brought some books, but it's so different and beautiful here, I want to experience that. I like the tranquillity. Sometimes I see some deer, or a raccoon."

He nodded. "Maybe I'll walk down with you, tonight. I haven't seen the lake yet except from the porch."

Sara's heart skipped a beat, then picked up its tempo. It was the first suggestion he'd made for them to spend some time together. Had he gotten over some of his anger about her keeping the baby a secret?

"If you like. I want to do the dishes first. It won't take long."

"I'll clear, you have to wash."

"I can manage." She rose and picked up her plate. He rose at the same time and picked up his. "You know our rule—that the person who cooked doesn't have to clean up. Obviously I can't do the dishes with the cast, but I can pull my own weight."

Sara nodded remembering when he'd first told her about the rule he and his father and brother had had. It had been one of the few snippets of information he'd given about his childhood. Normally Alec never spoke about his family and what she'd learned had been mostly from Wyatt.

Including the fact their mother had walked out when Alec had been five.

In light of her own situation, Sara could understand a woman leaving her husband—given enough provocation. Hadn't she done that very same thing? But to leave her babies? Never! Her heart went out to a little five-year-old boy who probably still wondered where his mother was and why she hadn't come home.

Did he still think about that?

Once the dishes were put away, Sara headed for the stairs. "I'll run up and get my jacket and be ready in a second."

"I can get it for you if you like. If you don't want to be taking stairs and all. In your condition, I mean."

She laughed softly. "Thanks, Alec, but exercise is the best thing for me. That's one reason I'm so excited about being here—I can take long walks to explore. I'm not sick, you know."

He frowned. "Should you be taking walks alone? What if you fell or something?"

"I watch where I'm going."

It was a bit too late for him to show concern.

By the time they'd reached the lake, Sara had herself in hand. Twice Alec had brushed against her as they followed the path from the cottage to the lakeshore. Each time that curious tingling had darted hither and yon, making her extremely conscious of the man beside her and of her own feminine reaction.

Not that anyone would be interested in her at this point. She'd not been able to keep Alec's attention when she wasn't eight months pregnant. But she almost relished the sensations. At least they showed she was alive and capable of being interested again. Maybe one day she would change her mind and let herself fall for another man, hard as it was to believe.

For now, it was enough to have companionship on her walk.

"Beautiful, isn't it?" she asked, when they came out of the trees and paused. The lake gleamed in the last rays of the sun. Almost as smooth as glass, it reflected the distant shore. Several boats still dotted the mirrored surface. The sound of laughter skipped across the water.

"Want to sit on the dock?" Sara asked impulsively. She headed for the wooden structure without waiting for a response. On the far side of the lake the main marina could be seen, lights coming on as twilight enveloped the earth.

Easing herself down on the edge, she dangled her feet over the side. They were still a foot or more above the water level.

Alec sat beside her. "Are you going to be able to get up again?"

She laughed, sheer joy in the tranquil evening filling her. "If not, you'll have to hoist me up like a derrick."

Tied to the right at the end of the dock was a small rowboat, and beyond it one of the two-seater paddle boats.

"One day I want to do the paddle boat," she said. "But I need a partner."

He studied it for a moment. "Wouldn't we swamp the thing? Isn't it for kids?"

"No, it's for whomever is staying at our cabins. And I've seen several adults out on the lake in them. I think it looks like fun."

"Fun? We'd probably get soaked, if we didn't capsize."

"We?" She laughed again. "I didn't say *you* had to be the partner."

Alec looked at her. "Who else is there?" He realized he didn't want her sharing the paddle wheel with anyone else.

Startled by the realization, he looked back at the paddle wheel. It looked like a toy, barely big enough to hold two adults. They'd be sitting hip to hip, shoulder to shoulder. Her sweet fragrance would envelop them. Her laughter would ring out with the joy she often displayed.

Which wouldn't be all bad, he mused. Maybe Wyatt was right. And the doctor. And Sara. Maybe he did need to broaden his parameters and discover what was out there beyond work.

"I'm game if you are," he said.

"You can't get your cast wet," she reminded him.

"Are you suggesting we can't master the craft? That we could end up in the lake?" he asked in mock indignation.

"You don't think there's the slightest possibility?"

He shook his head firmly.

"That water is cold. I've seen kids playing in it, but when I dipped my hand in yesterday, I don't know how they do it," she warned.

"Kids don't have a thermostat. I remember when Wyatt and I played in rivers that no one else would go in because they were so cold. We never noticed at the time."

"What were the two of you like as kids?" Secretly thrilled at the fact Alec was talking about his past, she almost held her breath lest he clam up.

"Hellions, if my dad's to be believed."

Sara leaned back on her hands and gazed over the water as she listened to Alec tell her some outlandish story about him and his brother. She loved listening to his voice. Closing her eyes, she focused on the intonation, the cadence. No wonder he did so well as a prosecuting attorney, his delivery was tremendous.

Suddenly he stopped. She opened her eyes and looked at him. He had his eyes closed.

"Are you all right?" She sat up and put her hand on his arm.

"Dizzy again. It comes and goes."

"Lie back down on the dock. When it passes, we'll head for the cabin."

Alec lay back and after a moment, Sara did as well. Stars were beginning to appear in the dark sky. Would they have trouble finding their way back? The path was so easy during the day. But neither had thought to bring a flashlight. And the tree canopy would cut off any illumination from overhead.

"Do these attacks happen often?" Sara asked.

"I was dizzy for an entire two days immediately following the accident, so there is definite improvement. But I'm not driving yet, or doing anything else that would cause complications if I get a spell," he said, his eyes firmly shut. "The doctor said they'll end before long. As soon as my head heals."

They fell silent and Sara let herself enjoy her hunt for stars and constellations she recognized. How long had it been since she'd done this? Stargazing wasn't a pastime she partook of in Boston.

"Actually I was thinking about what you said earlier," Alec said a moment later.

"About what?"

"About not working all the time. Maybe I'll join you on one of your walks. Even go with you out in that paddle boat."

# CHAPTER FOUR

SARA turned to look at him. It had grown so dark it was difficult to see clearly.

"Are you serious?"

"Sure. Why not?"

Reserving judgment, she thought about his suggestion. It would be nice to have someone to do a few things with, at least the things she couldn't do alone. And she was dying to try the paddle boats.

*Don't get your hopes up,* she warned herself. You know what Alec is like. He makes plans and doesn't keep them if work intrudes.

"I'll take you up on the paddle boats, but don't feel obligated. I planned to be here entirely on my own. I don't need someone to entertain me."

"Would you rather I didn't spend time with you?" he asked curtly.

"No," she said quickly, amazed to realize how much she wanted him to. "I guess I'm just surprised you think you can squeeze me in."

"I'm sure I can manage a paddle or walk."

The cynic in her wanted to ask him for how long, but she remained silent. Skeptical, but hopeful. Was she setting herself up for disappointment?

"I didn't realize it was so dark," Alec said, slowly sitting up, then standing.

"Feeling better?" she asked, tilting her head back to see him.

"The dizziness has passed. Ready to head back?"

"Maybe I will use that help," she said, wondering if she should scoot back from the edge of the dock before attempting to stand. The baby threw her balance off.

He reached down his good hand and effortlessly pulled her to her feet. He didn't release her, but stood close, crowding her, taking the air until Sara wondered how she was going to move. And where. Stepping backward was out of the question. Stepping forward would put her right up against Alec.

Her nerves began to hum. Her body yearned for his, for a fleeting touch of his hand, for a searing kiss that would ignite her passion and sweep her away. As it had been once upon a time.

"I'll be able to manage on my own again one day," she said, tugging gently on her hand, refusing to dwell on the thoughts and memories that crowded her mind.

They walked slowly, finding the path, then discovering how dark it was beneath the branches. Twice Sara stumbled, Alec caught her both times. After the second incident, he took her hand firmly in his.

"If we're going too fast, we'll slow down," he said. "No taking chances with my son or daughter."

Heart racing at his touch, Sara tried to concentrate on walking. His concern was for the baby, not her. But the sensations that danced along her arm belied that belief. It seemed the path had disappeared.

Instead of paying attention to the uneven track, every inch of her seemed attuned to the man at her side.

His hand was firm and warm. His grip reassuring. His unique scent mingled with that of the trees and the lake. She wanted to imprint the memory on her mind to bring out in the future. A stolen night. All the more special for being unexpected.

Sara was almost sorry when they reached the cottage. Reluctantly she released his hand to climb the three shallow steps leading to the porch. The door was unlocked. Switching on the living-room lamps a moment later, she felt blinded after the enclosing darkness.

She turned, surprised to find Alec so close. She smiled, hoping her nervousness wasn't obvious. Her heart seemed caught in her throat, racing out of control.

"I thought I'd take a long walk in the morning. Do you wish to go?" If he could make a gesture, so could she. "Or will that be when you work?" she asked quickly, hoping her voice sounded normal. She would not be disappointed if he said no!

"I'll catch up tonight, so tomorrow morning should be free."

Walking up the stairs seconds later, Sara had the feeling he'd already forgotten her presence. Totally focused on his laptop, Alec didn't seem to know anyone or anything else existed.

Don't expect anything to change, she warned herself as she closed her bedroom door. As someone to take an occasional ramble with, Alec might be fine. Any hope for more was strictly forbidden!

Unconsciously she raised her hand to her cheek, rubbing it absently against her skin. She could smell him on her palm. The awakening sensations in her body did not prove conducive for quickly falling asleep. But that's what she planned to do. No more thoughts of Alec or what might have been.

Time enough in the morning to see if he meant what he'd said. Not that she cared. She refused to let herself fall into that trap a second time. The two of them were sharing a cottage for a few short weeks and once her vacation was over, they'd go their separate ways.

The next morning when Sara descended the stairs, she was surprised to see Alec up and dressed and already hip deep in paper. He wrote on a yellow pad, sheets of paper on the sofa beside him, a stack on the coffee table and a few more pieces on the floor.

"Good morning," she called softly.

He glanced up and nodded, returning immediately to his notes.

So much for expecting companionship on her vacation, she thought wryly as she prepared pancakes for breakfast.

Sitting in solitary splendor a few minutes later, she began to eat, savoring each mouthful. As the minutes ticked by, she wondered if Alec had already eaten. Or if skipping meals was the norm for him.

Shades of their past.

Only this time she refused to get upset.

"Not good for either of us," she murmured, patting her stomach. Instead of fretting that the man was so caught up in business he ignored his own need for food, she planned her day. If Alec still wished to accompany her, fine. If not, she'd still go on her ramble—maybe try to walk around the lake.

Once finished, she washed her plate, tidied the kitchen and packed a lunch—with a bit more than she expected to eat, just in case. Finished, she pushed through the swinging door to the living room.

"I'm ready to leave. Are you still going with me?" she asked brightly before she realized he had his cell phone to his ear. On the phone already!

He looked up. "Hold on a minute, Teresa. What?"

"I'm going for that walk. I've packed a lunch. Are you still planning to go?"

"Yes. I'll be done here in a minute. Are you planning to eat breakfast first?"

"Already taken care of."

"Oh." He frowned.

If he thought she planned to feed him while he ignored her, he'd better think again!

"If you'll be ready soon, I'll have a cup of tea."

"Yes, I— What?" His attention again focused on the phone.

Sara went back to the kitchen and prepared a cup of herbal tea. Waiting twenty minutes while she sipped the fragrant brew, she gave up and left for her walk. Alone.

"Good morning, Sara, lovely day, isn't it?" Mrs. Simpson called as Sara passed their cottage on the way to the path to the lake.

"It's beautiful. I'm going to see if I can walk around the lake."

"That's ambitious. It seems quite a long way. Don't get too tired. Won't your husband be joining you?"

Sara smiled and tried to ignore the disappointment the thought brought. "Not today. He's working. If I get tired, I'll stop at the main lodge and have someone bring me back."

"Good plan. We hope to take one of those rowboats out today. Paul wants to try his hand at fishing. I told him that was fine, but he had to clean any we caught. Of course, if we're really lucky, we'll have enough for a fish fry and can invite you and the honeymooners over tomorrow night. Enjoy your walk, my dear."

Sara waved and set off. The morning was still cool enough that the sun felt good on her arms and face. She'd brought a hat to wear, but carried it in her backpack now, with her lunch. The silence was delightful. She could hear a few songbirds singing from the trees. The lake lapped gently along the shore, soothing and tranquil.

She would enjoy the day and not feel disappointed Alec was not with her. When she had arrived at the cabin, she had not expected to see him. There was no reason to feel short-changed that he preferred work to a walk.

But she did—because he'd said he'd come last night.

For a fleeting moment she'd thought he might have changed, that maybe the accident might have put things into a different perspective. Or that he might want to know about the baby.

So much for expecting a miracle.

Alec clicked off the phone and leaned back. The dizzy spell caught him unaware as always. Waiting patiently until it passed was difficult. He wasn't used to waiting for many things. How many more attacks would he have today? He should be keeping score. They were growing farther and farther apart, as the doctor said they would. But he still experienced far more than he wanted!

Slowly he became aware of the silence. Where was Sara? Shouldn't he hear her fussing around? Was she ready to go? As the dizziness faded he rose and went into the kitchen. It was empty.

Turning, he went back to the stairs. Her bedroom door was open, the room empty. There were few personal items evident, but her scent seemed to cling in the air—light and flowery. How had he missed it that first day? It seemed to be everywhere.

Suddenly he wanted to locate her. Take that walk, find something else to do besides reviewing the briefs that waited to be read, and dealing with the fax his secretary would be sending.

Sara wasn't on the porch.

He wondered if she'd gone without him. A glance at his watch confirmed it. It was almost noon! Where had the morning gone?

"Where it always does," he said gazing toward the lake. He pulled the door shut, and headed down the steps. Maybe he could spot her on the beach.

As he passed the neighboring cabin, the older woman he'd seen yesterday called a greeting. She was sitting on a rocking chair, with what looked like knitting in her lap.

"Good morning, finally finished your work?" she called.

He nodded, wondering how she'd known.

"Have you seen Sara?" he asked.

"She took off for a walk around the lake. You can't catch up, she left a couple of hours ago."

He frowned, an unexpected feeling of disappointment sweeping through. Until that second he hadn't realized how much he'd been looking forward to spending time with her. He'd told her last night he'd go with her, so why had she left without him?

"You might get a Jeep to the lodge and see if she's there yet. She said if she got tired, she'd stop when she reached the lodge. I hope she's not doing too much in her condition."

"Exercise is good for her, and I doubt she'd overdo it," he said. Not that Sara needed defending. His response came automatically, surprising him. Except for Wyatt when they were younger, Alec had never felt the need to defend anyone.

Upon reaching the resort a half hour later, Alec bypassed the lodge and headed directly for the lake. There was a wide sandy beach, complete with lifeguard. Children played in the water, parents swimming with them or watching from the shore.

He paused and surveyed the scene, feeling totally out of place. He looked for Sara. Couples and families were everywhere. The resort was perfect for that kind of thing but not so perfect for single people, he thought, feeling like an outsider. Even ones who came to recuperate and discovered their estranged wives.

He didn't see her. Spotting a couple of empty lounge chairs, he strode over and sat down. The sun felt good as he leaned back. Had she already passed by? How long would it take her to walk around half the lake?

He'd wait a little while before giving up. The urge to find her, to join her for at least some of the day, was surprisingly strong.

He'd meant what he'd said yesterday. He'd promised Wyatt he would try to relax, to find something else to entertain him besides work. Could Sara help—at least while he was here?

Alec was about to give up when he saw her. She was watching the children play as she walked slowly along the water's edge. He rose to intercept.

"I thought we were going to walk together," he said a minute later.

Sara stopped and looked up in surprise. "Alec. I didn't expect to see you." Exaggerating, she peered around him. "Where's your phone and laptop?"

"All right, I got caught up in the conversation. But you could have waited."

She shrugged. "I did. For twenty minutes. Then I gave up." She looked around. "Is there someplace to sit? I'm tired."

"I'm not surprised—trying to walk around the lake. It's huge. You should know better—especially in your condition."

"I managed this far."

"Yes, and you look wiped out. You need to take better care of yourself."

He took her arm and led her back to the chairs he'd just vacated. "You're doing too much."

"I can take care of myself," she said, pulling her arm away and sinking onto the chair. "I've managed for the last six months on my own. And the baby and I'll do great once it arrives."

He stood, fists on hip, studying her. She looked exhausted. Her eyes were already closed and she leaned back in the chair as if she wasn't planning to move again for a decade.

He didn't like her comment, didn't like being reminded she could manage her life fine without him.

"Did you eat lunch?"

"No. Not yet. I packed stuff in the backpack," she said, making no effort to open it.

"Sorry I wasn't ready to go when you were," he said stiffly. She could have waited a bit longer. Or reminded him she was waiting.

He sat beside her, admitting reluctantly that if she had waited, she'd have wasted her entire morning. If he'd meant what he'd said last night, why hadn't he rearranged things this morning?

"Oh!" Sara's eyes flew open and her hands went to her stomach.

"What's wrong?" He leaned closer, concern striking. "Is it the baby? Too much exertion?"

"No. It's just the baby's practicing to be a place-kicker, I think," she said. "I guess since he was quiet while I was walking, he now feels it's his turn."

"It's a boy?"

"I don't know. I just call the baby he. Could be a girl, I suppose."

"Do you want a son?" he asked. The entire concept of pregnancy and childbirth was foreign to him. Intriguing though. Imagine having a baby inside, a baby that one day would grow up to be a man or woman. A part of him and of Sara.

"I just want a healthy baby."

He could see the ripple beneath her cotton top as the baby kicked again. Amazing. He'd never been this close to a pregnant woman. What must it be like?

She tilted her head, staring at him. "Do you want to feel him move?"

His eyes met hers. For a long moment he gazed into the warmth of those brown eyes. Nodding, he reached out and placed his palm where hers had been. She covered his hand with hers and moved it slightly to the left.

Nothing happened.

Alec was about to remove his hand when he felt a definite kick. Stunned he couldn't move.

"That was quite a punch. Does it hurt?"

She smiled and shook her head. "Not really. Sometime it surprises me. There, feel it again?"

He nodded, struck by the warmth that seeped through him. He'd never experienced anything like it before. For a moment Alec felt as if he was poised on the brink of something wonderful, monumentally special. The sounds of the children's laughter and shrieks faded, the warmth from the sun seemed to fill every inch of his body. Sara's expression was ethereal, perfect for a mother.

When the baby settled down, she removed her hand from the back of his. Despite the warmth of the sun, Alec felt slightly chilled.

"I've been wanting to share that with someone since I first felt him move," she said, closing her eyes again. "I want to eat here," she said. "I'm too tired to move a step until I get some sustenance. Then I want to take a Jeep home and sleep until supper!"

He'd finished working for the day, but it looked as if he and Sara hadn't managed to connect. She'd done her outside activity and now wanted a nap. He'd finally carved out some free time, and had no one to share it with.

As if she'd read his mind, she opened her eyes and looked at him. "Something wrong?"

"No. I wouldn't mind eating myself, I missed breakfast."

She sat up and unzipped the backpack, withdrawing a wrapped sandwich and handing it to him—a thick roast beef one made with mustard and slightly wilted lettuce.

"Finished work for the day?"

"I have to pick up a fax before we leave the lodge. And check to see if a packet arrived by courier."

"Then that'll keep you busy this afternoon," she commented, turning to watch the kids frolicking in the water. "Unless you plan to take a nap, too. You are supposed to be recovering from the accident and getting rest."

Suddenly the thought of the two of them climbing the stairs together jumped into his mind. Images of

Sara in his arms, in a bed, danced before him. He could see settling her against his shoulder, placing his palm against her belly, feeling their baby move again before drifting to sleep.

He wanted to trace that silky skin with his fingertips. Thread his fingers through that soft hair and breathe in her unique fragrance. He'd love to just hold her. And then do more than just holding.

What would she do if he kissed her again? Slap his face? Ask for another? His anger with her had abated. The longing might never fade.

He grew uncomfortable and shifted slightly on the chair. Concentrate on eating and not sleeping, he admonished himself.

Sara finished her food and leaned back, feeling relaxed and replete. If she didn't get home soon, she'd fall asleep where she sat. It was all the fresh air and sunshine, she thought drowsily. And just maybe the walk had been too challenging for her.

But she hated to move. For the moment, at least, she had company. Alec had been quiet while eating, but she felt no impatience or restlessness.

Which meant what? That he was content to sit for a while before heading back to work? Or was he truly making an effort to explore other avenues while on his enforced vacation?

"The Simpsons might invite us to a fish fry tomorrow night," she said, remembering Mrs. Simpson's invitation. "You don't have to go, but right now the idea sounds appealing. I've visited several times with them over the past few days."

"They're the older couple in the cottage to the right?"

"Yes."

"She's the one who told me I might be able to intercept you here."

"Mmm."

"Come on, Sara, let's get you home." He reached out and took hold of her hand, tugging gently. "You're about to fall asleep."

She rose, all thought of sleep fleeing as she registered his touch. His hand held hers as if wasn't going to let go anytime soon. She remembered his holding her last night, and the way her body seemed to rev up anytime it came near him. The same thing was happening again!

When he picked up her backpack with his injured arm, she reached out to take it.

"Don't do that. You need to let it heal."

"The pack doesn't weigh that much."

"Still." She slung it over her shoulder and headed toward the lodge.

"Hello, enjoying the afternoon?"

It was Molly Harper, the abandoned wife from the first afternoon. Sara smiled and nodded, blushing slightly at the very pointed glance at their linked hands.

"Good for you! Bill's at it again. But he promised to quit by four today. You and your husband enjoy yourselves." With a gay wave, Molly headed for the beach, book tucked in hand, towel slung over her shoulder.

Sara looked at Alec, expecting a reaction. She was surprised to see the amusement in his eyes.

"I should have set her straight the other day," she said wryly.

He raised their hands. "She'd just think something was going on."

"Hardly likely, given my condition."

"What are you talking about?"

"Just look at me!" she said, pausing and turning to face him.

"I do look at you. I'd look a lot longer but didn't think good manners would permit."

She blinked. Had that been a compliment? No, she'd imagined it. Alec didn't give compliments.

Two minutes later he was conversing with the front desk clerk, picking up a folder and a large envelope. More work. At least she wouldn't worry she'd miss any stunning change while she napped!

When Sara awoke, it was late afternoon. She felt pleasantly relaxed, still a bit tired. The walk had been more than she should have undertaken. Thank goodness she'd been able to get a ride home from the main lodge.

She listened intently. No voices. Did that mean Alec was not on his phone?

A few minutes later she confirmed her conclusion. He was again fast asleep on the sofa, papers scattered everywhere. Spotting the phone, she picked it up and turned it off. He needed rest, not more problems.

Did he think the legal structure of the entire city of Boston would come to a screeching halt if he weren't working full-out? Weren't there a dozen or more assistant district attorneys? The others could cover his workload until he returned.

She placed the phone on the table and wandered onto the porch. Mr. Simpson was almost at the cabin.

"Howdy, young lady. The missus sent me over to tell you and your husband dinner is on us tomorrow night. You come about seven."

"So you caught a lot of fish."

He beamed and nodded. "They practically jumped into the boat. With what I'm sure to catch tomorrow, we'll have more than enough for all of us, and those honeymooners if we can tear them away from each other long enough to eat." He touched two fingers to his forehead in a casual salute and headed on to the Martins's cabin.

Sara watched him, suddenly realizing she wanted to go to dinner and hadn't a clue if Alec would accompany her or not.

She couldn't help remembering another dinner she'd asked him to attend. The annual event sponsored by her company. The one in which she was given that bonus and accolades for exceptional work on the Crenshaw project.

His absence had been the final straw. She'd packed up and moved out the next morning.

# CHAPTER FIVE

"I THOUGHT I heard voices," Alec said behind her as he stepped out onto the porch.

Sara looked over her shoulder.

"Mr. Simpson stopped by, extending that invitation to dinner tomorrow evening."

That catch in her heart caught her by surprise again. It seemed to happen every time she saw him. Taking a deep breath, she tried to regain a feeling of tranquillity.

"And that has you upset?" he asked, his eyes narrowed as he studied her expression.

"No." Her face flamed. She would never be good at subterfuge. Neither did she wish to bring up the missed dinner six months ago. There was no sense rehashing past mistakes.

"Actually, I, um, didn't know if I should have accepted for you. His invitation caught me by surprise. I didn't have a chance to think before he was heading off to the other cottage to invite the honeymooners."

"I like fish. You mentioned the honeymooners before. Who are they?"

"James and Hilary Martin. They've been married, let's see, it will be eight or nine days now. And if you ask, they'll tell you down to the minute." She smiled ruefully. "They are so crazy in love."

"Um," he said, leaning against the porch support and gazing toward the gleam of water. "That won't last."

Sara's smile faded. "No, it won't, will it, according to you. Wait until the reality of life slams them in the face."

Alec slanted her a look.

"Just because what we had wasn't the kind of love that lasts a lifetime doesn't mean others can't find it," Sara continued. "Wait until you see the Simpsons. They are in their late seventies, and have been married more than fifty years. You can feel the love surrounding them. Just because what we had didn't last doesn't mean love isn't real or doesn't exist. Look at Wyatt and Elizabeth—it's obvious others experience it."

"But not you and me?"

"I can't speak for you, Alec, but I hope to find a deep and abiding love one day. A lasting love, a feeling of completeness and desire to share my life with one special person. It wasn't you, but that doesn't mean I'm giving up or resigning myself to living alone forever." Brave words, which she wasn't sure she meant. For the time being she was too scared of being hurt again.

"You won't be alone. You'll have the baby," he reminded her.

"Yes, and I'll love this child like crazy. But I also want an adult love, someone to share my life with. Is that such a hard concept?"

"Isn't that what we tried? You walked out, not me. My mother walked out on my old man. If that's what love does, I don't want any part of it. I gave it a shot, but it didn't work."

Sara took a deep breath and tried to damp down the anger that rose. "I left, but our marriage was over long before, Alec. I could argue that you were already gone. And I don't know what happened between your father and mother. I expect you don't know the full story—only the two of them know it all. But don't you think one day you'll regret spending your entire life alone—focused exclusively on work? What about a family? How much time will you devote to your son or daughter? Will you want to share holidays with the baby? What about a shoulder to lean on when things get tough?"

"I have Wyatt for family. And I can stand alone if things get tough. Isn't that what you're doing?"

She shook her head. "You think I'm on my own because I came here to be alone. But I have a mother who is very supportive. I have several very close friends. Cousins who would help out in a minute. But I still want that special someone—"

"Some man to come in and sweep you off your feet?" The sarcasm bit.

She laughed aloud. "Alec, that's so dumb. Men don't sweep women off their feet anymore. I'm talking about a partnership. I'll bring something to the relationship as will he. And together we'll have that special relationship—like the Simpsons. When you see them together, you'll be so amazed. They remind me of honeymooners even after fifty years."

"You'd better make sure they know up-front we

are not going to be holding hands and making eyes at each other!''

Sara turned away, nodding her head in agreement. Even when they were dating, Alec didn't hover. He was nothing like James Martin who seemed to be constantly touching Hilary. Wistfully she wished he were.

But at least he was going to the dinner. She just hoped it wouldn't prove awkward.

A pang hit that their marriage had not stood the test of time. That the love and caring she'd had for the man had not been enough to bridge the differences between them.

"I'm going in," she said, wanting time alone. Needing time away from him before his proximity had her imagining things that would never again be.

When Sara and Alec walked to the next cottage just before seven the next evening, Sara was surprised to see a wooden picnic table set up near the back door of the cottage, fully set for dinner. Nearby a portable barbecue unit was already glowing with coals.

"Welcome." Mrs. Simpson bustled out of the house to greet them.

"This is nice," Sara said, waving at the table.

"We called the front desk and they arranged everything. This is really a wonderful resort. They claim to have everything and so far, I believe them! They'll pick it up tomorrow, unless we wish to keep it to eat out on from time to time while we're here. I thought this would be much nicer than eating inside. Come and sit down."

"Mrs. Simpson, I don't know if you met Alec," Sara began.

"Oh, call me Rosemarie. And my husband is Paul. Nice to meet you, Alec. What can I get you to drink? Paul has some beer, and there's wine, or soft drinks," she said smiling at Sara.

They were barely settled with drinks when James and Hilary Martin strolled up. Rosemarie made hasty introductions and hurried off to get their beverages.

Hilary smiled and snuggled closer to James. "How lovely to be expecting a baby. We want children, but not right away. We want to spend sometime together first. How long have you two been married?"

"Eighteen months," Alec stated baldly.

Sara looked at him, waiting for the rest. He flicked her a glance, then looked back at the Martins. He wasn't going to tell them their marriage was over? At least not mentioning it took care of any awkwardness. And it was true. They had married almost eighteen months ago—lived as man and wife for twelve of those months and had been separated for six.

Sara changed the subject. By the time the first platter of fish was placed in the center of the table, all reservations had fled and the three couples chatted as if they'd known each other for years—despite the differences in age.

Twice, Sara fell quiet to watch Alec. She'd missed him. Missed hearing him talk, laughing at his dry humor, and watching him argue points he was trying to make. James had to be at least six or seven years younger than Alec and Paul Simpson was a good forty plus years older. Yet the three men had plenty to say, often arguing, but Sara suspected that was Alec's doing, since he reveled in it.

It was late when the party broke up. Sara wondered if they'd do something like this again before the others left. It had been a delightful evening. She liked people and was glad the neighboring cottages had such congenial couples staying in them.

"Did you enjoy yourself?" she asked as they stepped onto the porch.

"Yes. I could tell you were having fun, too."

She was struck by the fact he'd noticed. "I had a great time! I noticed except for one or two comments, you didn't talk about your work at all. Don't you feel you're suffering from withdrawal?" she teased, stalling. She hated for the evening to end. For a few hours Alec had been the man she remembered. Attentive, attractive and amusing. She hated to let it go.

"Want to sit out for a while, or are you tired?"

"I'm not tired. I'm still revved up from the conversation, I guess. Plus, I rested earlier. How about you?"

"I'm fine."

"Are you getting enough rest, Alec? You're still working even though you are supposed to be on vacation."

"I'm fine, Sara. I don't need a keeper."

His quiet voice held a note of steel in it. Sara blinked.

"Of course you don't. And if you did, I'm not applying for the job!"

He was silent and Sara tried to relax. It was difficult when she was so aware of him. She could easily reach out and touch him, if she dared. She thought she had gotten over Alec during the months they'd been apart. Now she was starting to wonder if she had been fooling herself.

Crossing her arms over her chest, she clenched her hands into fists to resist temptation. What was the matter with her? They had tried love and marriage. It hadn't worked and it was time to let go and move on!

"Cold?"

"No."

"Tell me, do you plan to continue work when the baby is born?" he asked.

"After the first few months, yes. I have a long maternity leave, but I love my job."

"So you don't believe a woman should stay home with her children?"

"Not necessarily. My mother always worked, and I think I turned out okay. The reality is how the relationship works when we're together. This baby will be a very important part of my life. I'll take the best care of it!"

He leaned his head back. Sara thought he'd closed his eyes, but it was too dark to see him clearly. Was he having another dizzy spell?

"Are you all right, Alec?" she asked, growing concerned.

"I'm still trying to come to terms with a baby on the way."

Truth to tell, she wondered if she hadn't wanted

to share her precious baby with a man who put work before all else. She wanted her son or daughter to know it was loved. But she had robbed Alec of the chance to share in the joy.

"Are you mad about the baby?"

"No!" He was silent a moment, then said, "But I am still hurt you didn't tell me when you first knew."

"I guess I had some outdated notion you'd think we needed to live together if I told you. And there is nothing you can do before it's born."

"We'll never know, now, will we?"

"Tell me," she said, ruthlessly changing the subject, "is this your idea of a relaxing vacation, scrambling to do things on the phone or via fax or the computer, rather than going into the office?"

"Not your idea of relaxing, huh?"

"Definitely not. You need lessons in how to relax. Do you want to go hiking with me tomorrow?" She waited for his answer with some trepidation. While she still felt pumped up from the delightful dinner, she knew she ran a certain risk in inviting him.

"Didn't yesterday's trek tire you out?"

"Yes, but today's rest perked me right up and I'm raring to go again. Only this is the last time I ask. If you don't keep this appointment, I cross you off my list!"

"I promise to be ready to leave when you are."

For a moment Sara wanted to ask why he had not been able to make such a promise when they were together.

"Is this another attempt to circle the lake?" he asked.

"No. There are some paths leading back toward the hills, I thought we could hike up and see if there's a view."

"Sounds strenuous."

"No, easy enough for a pregnant lady. I checked with the front desk. I'm not talking rock climbing. How about you?"

"Wherever a pregnant lady can go, I can go. Fix a picnic and we'll eat it while enjoying that fabled view."

"If we find one."

He rolled his head toward her. "Actually I could just look at you and enjoy the view."

Heat swept through her at his words. She lost her train of thought. Alec had never been one to give compliments. How she cherished this one!

Feeling flustered, Sara didn't know how to respond. "What a nice thing to say."

"It's true. You are a beautiful woman, Sara. I don't think I fully appreciated that before."

Stunned, she tried to see him in the faint starlight. Only his silhouette was visible.

"It's getting late." Great, run away, she thought, unsettled. What she really wanted to do was to stay and see if he'd say something more!

"And we'll want an early start," he said, rising. Holding his hand for her, he clasped hers when she offered it and pulled her gently to her feet.

Only he didn't let go. Sara felt tongue-tied. She tried to discern his expression, but it was too dark.

"Good night," she said softly, wondering if that would release her from the spell.

"Good night, Sara." He didn't move. Didn't release her. But his head seemed to be coming closer. Was he planning to kiss her?

Her heart skipped a beat and began a frantic tattoo. Panic flared. She hadn't been kissed in months except for his angry kiss that first day! Was she ready for this?

Sidestepping to her left, she tugged her hand free.

"I'll make a picnic lunch tomorrow. But be warned, I'm leaving right at nine."

"I'll be ready."

Was there a thread of amusement in his tone? Sara didn't stop to analyze it, she opened the door and practically ran up the stairs.

By the next morning she had put the evening in perspective. Alec was sharing her cabin while on vacation. And he had agreed to go on a hike today. Nothing more.

The thought of his kissing her had been a figment of her imagination. She'd ignore her flight of fancy and concentrate on why she'd come to the resort— to figure out what the next step should be. While they were both here, she should bring up the matter of a divorce. They could discuss it like rational adults.

But the thought of actually having a conversation that would end her marriage for all time almost made her sick. She had wanted so much from their marriage and hated the fact nothing had turned out the way she'd dreamed. Stalling didn't change things, but it gave her some kind of hope. Foolish that it might prove to be.

Maybe one day she'd meet another man to fall in love with, but she couldn't imagine it right now. How would she ever forget Alec?

He was not in the living room when she went downstairs. She saw no sign of him and wished she'd noticed if his bedroom door had been shut. Was it possible he hadn't woken yet?

She prepared coffee and herbal tea, then began making French toast. It was quick and easy to prepare. To her surprise, the back door opened just as she placed the first egg-drenched piece of bread in the pan.

"Good morning," Alec said, closing the door behind him. He carried his computer in his left hand.

"Hi, you're up and out early." She turned her attention to the cooking bread, trying to ignore how her heart had leaped when he walked in. Her hand shook a bit and she pressed her lips together tightly. She was *not* getting any ideas about their relationship!

"I jotted some notes after you went to bed last night and then wanted to send them to my secretary so she can get working on it today."

"You've been to the lodge already?"

He nodded. "Clearing the decks, so to speak. I'm ready for that hike now."

"Good." The glow of happiness that spread was not to be ignored, though Sara tried. She felt like a kid in a candy shop—she'd have Alec to herself for hours!

He placed the computer on the table and walked over to stand beside her. Too close, Sara wanted to say, but remained silent, trying to concentrate on the bread browning in the pan and not notice how her entire body seemed to be attuned to his.

She longed to turn around and talk to him, find out every drop of information she could about what he'd been doing over the last six months. Find out more about the accident. Get him to talk so she could listen to his voice. She'd missed him so much!

"Sara."

She turned and bumped into him. Reaching out, she steadied herself. His warmth enveloped her. She could feel the hard muscles beneath her fingertips. Her gaze caught with his and endless minutes seemed to pulse by. When she dropped her gaze to his mouth, she felt her heart accelerate out of control.

Slowly he lowered his head and kissed her. His lips were warm, gentle and oh so familiar.

It was brief—too brief, Sara thought wildly when he raised his head. She wanted more!

Her gaze locked with his.

"I've been wanting to do that since I first saw you," he said, still only inches away. His breath fanned across her heated cheeks. "That first kiss wasn't what I wanted. I was furious with you, and took it out in the kiss."

Licking her lips nervously, she tried to smile, but her face muscles didn't seem to work. "Yes, I know. This kiss was nice. I wouldn't mind another one."

Alec gathered her against him and covered her mouth with his. This kiss was not warm and gentle, but hot and wild. And when his tongue teased against her lips, she parted them to give him access to her mouth eagerly meeting him in the remembered dance of passion.

The earth seemed to spin, blood pounded in her veins, and the heat mingled and melded and seemed to pour fire through her. She could feel the plaster cast like an iron bar against her back, the rock hardness of his chest against her breasts and swollen belly. His hair was thick and surprisingly silky as her fingers tangled in it.

He tasted like coffee and fresh air and Alec. She had never felt quite like this. It was glorious. If it could only—

The baby kicked.

They broke apart, Alec's gaze dropped to her stomach.

"Well, I guess he made his feelings known," he said. "Was I holding you too tightly?"

Rubbing the rippling as the baby seemed to turn over, she shook her head. "No. He's just active about this time of morning."

Slowly Alec reached out his good hand and covered the mound. Sara laced her fingers through his as her palm covered the back of his hand and moved it slightly to where the baby was stretching. For long moments they didn't move, just shared the moment as their baby shifted.

Smoke wafted by.

"Oh, no. The toast!" Quickly Sara turned to the pan. The two slices of French toast smoked heavily.

She scooped them out and dumped them on a plate. They were as black as charcoal.

"Darn it! I wasn't paying attention."

"It's not as if we're on a schedule, right?" Alec said moving away. "I'll put the computer away and be back in a few minutes." He hesitated by the door. "Do you have enough for two?"

When she smiled and nodded, he left quickly. He had to get away before he did something foolish like swing her up in his arms and take her upstairs to bed! And that was the last thing she'd want.

He deposited his laptop on the sofa and went to stand on the front porch. It was still chilly, so maybe the crisp air would cool him down. Leaning against the porch support, he crossed his arms. He hadn't felt that strong sexual attraction around anyone except Sara. Despite their months apart, despite knowing he hadn't been able to keep his wife, he still wanted her.

He wanted to see the passion in her eyes from their kisses, from his touching her everywhere. Yearned to discover all the changes in her body, to explore the altered shape until he was as familiar with her now as he had been when they lived together.

He wanted to make love to his wife!

Taking a deep breath, he gazed off at the lake. Maybe a quick run around the perimeter was needed. Followed by a plunge into the icy water!

Yeah, and miss their hike?

No way! He was looking forward to the walk. The woods were pretty, the air crisp and clear. Since he hadn't had a vacation in years, it wouldn't hurt to try to relax as his doctor and Wyatt had so convincingly pointed out.

"Breakfast is ready."

He spun around. She stood in the doorway, a wary expression around her eyes.

He tried to smile. How did a man go about looking harmless? Especially when just the sight of her had him thinking things she'd be shocked to know. Like how he wanted to brush his fingers through her short hair, and kiss her again. How he longed to nibble the slender column of her neck. Or how his palms itched to feel the weight of her breasts, the roundness of her stomach.

"Then let's eat." He'd put all those thoughts firmly away—at least until he was alone and could give full rein to the fantasy of the two of them together.


It was after nine when they left the cottage. Taking the narrow trail leading from behind the cabin, they were soon enclosed in a world of green. The trees met overhead several times, shading the trail completely. Birds trilled in the branches, sunlight dappled the path and the air was hushed and still cool. In spots the path was narrow, and they went single file. When they stepped into a meadow they walked side by side.

Sara gazed around eagerly.

"Isn't it lovely?" she said. "If it were later, we could have our picnic here."

Alec stopped her, his hand on her shoulder.

"Look," he said softly, pointing to the far side.
Three deer grazed.

"Oh." She didn't move, studying the scene with
delight. Closing her eyes, she tried to imprint everything on her mind so she'd never forget. The weight
of Alec's hand, the warmth of the sun, the scent of
the air, and the tranquillity of the meadow.

Opening her eyes she smiled. "They're so sweet."

"Um," he said. "Ready to go?"

"Don't you want to watch them?"

"We saw them, maybe we'll see something else."

With a lingering look at the deer, Sara nodded and
began walking again. Their movement startled the
deer and in less than a second they'd disappeared
into the trees. The rustle of underbrush the only
sound of their passing.

"You must be paying more attention than I am,"
Sara commented as they ambled across the meadow.
"I wouldn't have seen them if you hadn't pointed
them out."

"Comes from paying close attention to juries. I
want to make sure they're on my wavelength when
arguing a case. Of course when Wyatt and I were
younger, we spent a lot of time outdoors, playing
pirates or cowboys and Indians."

"I can't imagine you doing that. Wyatt, maybe,
but not you."

"And why not? I was a great pirate!"

Sara laughed.

Alec stopped and swung her around, capturing her
in his arms. "I always found the treasure. But that

was kids' stuff. Now I'm older and I know what pirates really wanted.''

Pressed against him from thigh to breast, Sara knew what pirates wanted, too. The same thing she wanted.

Astonished at her thoughts, she pushed back. She would shock him if he ever suspected where her imagination was leading. She was certainly not in the proper shape to be attractive. Already feeling like a pumpkin, she knew she'd only get worse during the final weeks.

"Dazzling damsels who would lure them away from their pirate ships?" she asked, catching her breath. Laughter danced in Alec's eyes. For the first time since she could remember he looked completely relaxed. The hike had been perfect for loosening him up and helping him unwind.

"You're dazzling," he said, reaching to clasp her hand in his and starting to walk again.

"Hardly." But her heart skipped another beat.

By the time they stopped, they'd crested a small knoll and discovered a great view of the lake. Sara was breathing hard, but felt exhilarated. She was no more tired than normal and, except for the last stretch, which had been fairly steep and rock strewn, the hike had been easy.

"I'm ready to stop, how about you?" Alec asked with a sideways glance at her.

"Yes, and I'm starving. Lunch now?"

"Good idea." He took off the backpack and looked around for a flat area without rocks. "Here?" he asked a minute later. Sara nodded and before long they were sitting on the large old blanket, eating and gazing at the view.

A slight breeze had her hair dancing, it felt good against her overheated skin. She'd shed her sweater on the last stretch and liked the warmth of the sun on her arms.

Alec watched her as she nibbled on the sandwich. She was beautiful. She always had been. How had he forgotten? Her eyes seemed to constantly sparkle with enthusiasm and joy. Her skin looked inviting, begging him to touch. Her mouth—he looked away, thinking how much he wanted to kiss her again. He balled the remains of his sandwich in the plastic and tossed it back into the backpack. He didn't want any more to eat. He wanted Sara.

Wanted to let his lips and tongue relearn every secret she held. Feel the warmth from her body pour into his. Taste her, touch her, lose himself in her.

He leaned back, gazing at the view, exquisitely conscious of the woman beside him.

"For a pirate, you're awfully quiet," she teased, repacking the remains of lunch and offering him a bottle of water.

He took it and drank deeply, handing it back. She smiled uncertainly.

It released the last constraint. Slowly, giving her time to refuse if she wished, he leaned forward until his mouth hovered scant millimeters from her own.

"Sara," he said softly, closing the distance and covering her lips with his.

She was warm and sweet, and very willing. As he followed her down until they were laying on the blanket, he never broke contact, his mouth opening to find the enchantment in hers.

Sara could scarcely breathe. She had not expected this, though in the fleeting seconds of rational thought remaining, she knew instinctively this is what she wanted.

Encircling Alec's neck, she reveled in the feel of his body pressing against hers, delighted in the sensations that exploded. His lips moved and she answered. His embrace tightened and she responded.

Her blood heated, rushed through her veins. The kaleidoscope of colors behind her lids added to the mesmerizing spell his touch wrought.

Endless moments slipped by, but Sara didn't count them. She kissed him back, letting her fingers relearn the texture of his hair, the steely strength of his muscles, the heat of his skin. Her fingers tingled, her body seemed unable to contain a myriad of sensations that struggled for dominance—heat, and desire, and love.

When his hand moved down her back and around to cup one breast, she caught her breath. Sensitized due to pregnancy, she felt the touch to her toes. Slowly his fingers moved beneath her loose top, skimming across her bare skin, holding her gently, his thumb rubbing across the tip. She longed for more, for his mouth to move there. Moving to allow him access, she deepened the kiss, trying to tell him without words she welcomed his touch. It had been so long.

Alec felt a wave of dizziness. Was it intoxication with Sara? Her scent filled him, her touch set him on fire. Her taste was so familiar, causing feelings and emotions to whirl without stop.

No. He opened his eyes, frowning as the dizziness didn't diminish.

Softly he groaned, clenched his teeth.

"Alec?" She opened her eyes and gazed up at him, looking more beautiful than a man could stand.

"Dammit," he said softly, closing his eyes and rolling to his side.

She rose up on one elbow, her expression concerned. "Alec, are you all right?" A hint of panic touched her voice.

"Dizzy spell again," he bit out. He hated this weakness. How much longer would they come?

"Can I do something? Get you something? Want some water?"

"I'll be fine once it passes."

"It's the first one today, isn't it?" she asked softly, her fingers brushing across his forehead. Alec wanted to capture her hand, bring it to his lips, lace his fingers through hers and hold hands. But it reminded him of the weakness. He couldn't even kiss his wife without repercussions from the accident.

The dizzy spells were affecting his common sense. He was not the hand-holding type.

"First one today," he confirmed.

"They're not frequent, then. Maybe they'll stop altogether soon," she said soothingly. "Maybe you should see a doctor again, just to make sure."

"I'll be fine."

"I'm worried about you,"

"Don't be. This is only temporary."

She was quiet and he rolled his head to the left squinting through one eye to see her. "Don't frown, you'll get wrinkles," he said, noting her worried expression. Despite all her animosity toward him, toward the situation he'd created, she still worried about him. A strange feeling settled around his heart.

"We'll wait until you feel completely better before heading back," she said practically, sitting up and running her fingers through her short hair.

"Didn't you say earlier there were caves around here?" Alec asked, hating being less than one hundred percent—especially around Sara. If he couldn't have her respect and regard, he sure didn't want her pity. His hands still felt the satiny texture of her skin, the weight of her breast, changed due to the pregnancy. He wanted more.

"Yes, a bit farther on, I think. Safe ones, the brochure said, not too deep, no long falls to some subterranean caverns by careless hikers. Why, do you want to explore them, Black Beard?"

He nodded, closing his eyes as a wave of nausea swept through. That was the worst of the dizziness—not only could he not keep his equilibrium, but he felt sick with it.

"But not today."

"We'll come back and explore them all, then," she said, lying back down. "I'm tired."

"Go to sleep. We aren't going anywhere anytime soon."

Neither spoke of the wild kisses, but he knew she was thinking about what just happened. Maybe she'd bring it up once he was fit again.

# CHAPTER SIX

ALEC woke and gazed around, feeling disoriented. For a moment he didn't remember where he was. A vague sense of unease filled him. He had to make sure Thompson didn't cut any deals with Snelling's attorney. This time Snelling was going up for a long stretch. Had he told Teresa to have that law clerk search for precedents for the Cannady case?

Damn, there was so much to do.

Then he saw Sara. She was still sleeping.

The dizziness was gone. He rose up on his elbow and studied her. She slept on her side. Her long lashes rested on her cheeks, and one hand pillowed her head. The short hair fell away from her forehead as the breeze teased it.

He wanted to kiss her awake. Take up where they'd been interrupted. Forget about work for a while, forget about their past and probable future, and live in the moment.

He watched her for a long time, wondering if this was all he was to have.

Checking his watch, he noted it was growing late. If he wanted to get hold of Teresa before she left today, they needed to head back. So much for the idyllic afternoon alone.

Wryly he admitted feeling refreshed from the nap, and from spending hours outside. Gazing off to the distant glimmer of the lake, he realized he had not thought about his caseload once until now. Unheard of!

It was Sara's spell. She had a way of weaving magic until he could think of nothing but her.

Well, he'd done his bit of vacation today. Time to get back and at least touch base with Teresa, make sure he continued to direct his pending cases. If he had to go to court in a few weeks' time, he wanted to be a part of the entire preparation process, not go in cold.

But for all the sense of urgency, of time wasting, he was reluctant to wake Sara. She looked so peaceful and perfect sleeping trustingly beside him. For the first time he wondered what the future would hold for her and their baby.

And for himself.

Where had they gone wrong? He'd thought a wife was supposed to stand by her husband's side. He'd been working for her—to afford nice things, a bigger apartment, nice cars.

And wouldn't the baby need a father? He and Wyatt had done without a parent most of their lives, and even today he felt the bitter loss. He was determined his child would know it was loved by both its parents—even if they couldn't live together.

Scowling, disliking the trend of his thoughts, he reached out and shook her lightly.

"Sara, wake up. We need to head back."

He couldn't help being entranced with the woman slowly coming awake. Her eyes looked large and dreamy. The cheek she'd been lying on was rosy, the other, pale. When she stretched, he almost held his breath. Except for the swelling of her stomach, the rest of her was slender and feminine, curved in all the right places.

He looked away, angry at the pull of attraction he didn't seem to be able to control. Wishing the memories didn't flood his mind. Wishing he felt he had the right to take up where they'd left off.

"It's not late, is it?" she asked rising slowly to her feet. Brushing off her jeans, she glanced at the sky, then at Alec, then away, as if unwilling to meet his gaze.

So much for a fantasy where she leaned over to kiss him again. Reluctantly he rose, reached down to fold the blanket.

"It's midafternoon. I want to get back to call the office."

"Well, of course. Why did I think you planned to spend the entire day relaxing?" Her sharp tone pierced him. Hadn't he spent hours with her? And enjoyed himself.

He swore he could feel her withdrawal. She said nothing, simply stood searching the area as he folded the blanket. But it was as if a wall had risen between them.

"Sara," he began. Then stopped. What was there to say? Hadn't they said all they had to say long ago?

"What?"

"Nothing. Are you ready?"

She shrugged and looked longingly at the hills rising behind them. "I told you about the caves, didn't I?"

"Yes. Maybe we can explore them another day."

"We're here now. They aren't far."

Alec looked at his watch again and shook his head. "It'll take us at least an hour to get back to the cabin, we need to leave now."

She met his gaze at last, her eyes grave. "So go. You're the one who wants to return. I'm going to the caves. I'll be back in time for supper." She turned and began walking toward the path that led higher.

"Sara, wait. You can't go up there alone."

Looking at him over her shoulder, she asked, "Why not?"

"It's not safe."

"I'm not going to take any risks. I just want to see the caves. The person at the front desk assured me it is safe. They wouldn't endanger their customers."

"I don't have time to go with you, I need to get back."

"No one is asking you to go with me, Alec."

With that, Sara turned and began walking along the path leading upward.

She carefully followed the trail, listening for any sound behind her that indicated Alec had changed his mind and had followed. Only silence met her ears, and the sound of her own footsteps. Disappointed, she tried to recapture the feeling she'd had earlier. He'd kissed her, and she didn't know how to react. Maybe if he'd awakened her with another kiss, she'd have had a clue. But he acted as if nothing had happened.

Maybe to him it meant nothing.

Shaking off her confusion, Sara tried to enjoy the beauty of the forest, to spot more deer, or a squirrel.

But her disappointment grew.

"Not that I expect him to spend every moment with me, but after those kisses, I guess I envisioned at least the rest of the day. Surely his almighty work could manage one full day without his august presence," she muttered.

She had only herself to blame for her feelings. She *knew* workaholics never changed. She had only deluded herself he wanted to spend time with her. She wouldn't make that mistake again! She had come on this vacation expecting to be alone. The fact he'd accompanied her on one walk was a bonus. But she wouldn't expect a repeat in the future.

By the time Sara returned to the cottage it was after seven. Pleasantly tired, she knew it was too late to fix an elaborate meal. She'd wash up and then fix an omelet or something.

Entering, she knew instantly the place was empty. Alec would be in the living room on the phone, surely, if he were home. He must still be at the lodge.

Taking a quick shower, she dressed in a loose-fitting dress. It was growing cool, but after wearing jeans all day, she was tired of the constriction. Slipping on a sweater against the growing evening chill, she went back downstairs.

Preparing herself a quick omelet, she ate in solitary silence, reading the new mystery she'd brought with her. Cleanup was minimal and when she finished, she wandered into the living room.

It seemed as if she'd spent little time in it since Alec had commandeered the room. Even now it was evident he considered it his office away from home. Papers were stacked in neat piles covering the coffee table and several areas on the floor. At least the sofa was clear, she thought, as she sat back and stretched out her legs. In only minutes, she was engrossed in her novel.

Alec returned some time later. She looked up in surprise when he entered the cabin, trying to ignore the catch in her heart. She was becoming used to it whenever she saw him. It meant nothing.

"I wondered where you were," she said lightly, marking her place in the book.

"I guess I should have called. I was longer at the lodge than expected. How were the caves?"

She nodded. "Interesting. Some were very shallow, but a couple were deep enough that it was dark in the back. Almost spooky. Next time I want to take a flashlight so I can explore more."

"Next time, I'll go with you."

She let the comment pass.

He dropped his laptop and briefcase near the door, and hesitated, as if unsure what to do next. Sara watched him without saying a word. He caught her gaze. He looked tired.

"Want some tea or something?" he asked. "I could use a cup of coffee."

"Thank you, that would be lovely," Sara said as she rose to follow him into the kitchen. "You seem to have an unlimited store of energy, working so long after our hike today."

He shrugged. "I had energy earlier, now I'm bushed."

"Did you have another dizzy spell?" She paused at the kitchen door, leaning against the jamb, watching him prowl around the kitchen.

He frowned. "Just a brief one at the lodge."

"Did you ever think your body is telling you to slow down?" she asked.

"No. I don't want to talk about it."

She sighed softly at the macho image men insisted on portraying. She was concerned for him—as she would be for anyone she knew.

In only a short time he had prepared two mugs. When he handed her one, she felt the brush of his fingertips as if they were charged with electricity. A shiver raced through her. Turning abruptly, she returned to the sofa, sitting in one corner, memories of that afternoon dancing in her memory. She wished she could sip the tea to give her something to do, but it was still far too hot.

Not that she was that much cooler. The images of their kisses, caresses, filled her. She glanced at Alec then away. What if he kissed her again tonight? What if she responded as she had, with abandon, with passion and desire. Shouldn't being pregnant damp down some of that?

What if *she* kissed *him!*

The idea tantalized. He wouldn't push her away, would he? She knew interest when she saw it, or felt it, as she had that afternoon. Of course she knew she could never compete with his work.

But one kiss. What could that hurt? For old times' sake?

Was she crazy? The man had proved he wasn't into long-term commitments, or love.

She glanced at him from beneath her lashes, shocked to find he was staring at her.

"You look pretty in that dress," he said.

Heat swept through, and her heartbeat increased. His compliments threw her.

"Thank you," she replied primly, bringing a gleam of amusement to his eyes.

Taking a sip of tea for courage, she deliberately placed the cup on a narrow open spot on the coffee table and turned to Alec, licking her lips in nervousness.

His expression didn't change, but she felt as if the air became supercharged. Could she do this?

How much did she want another kiss?

Daringly she reached out and took the cup from his hand, placing it beside hers. Taking a deep breath for courage, she looked at him, and scooted closer. Turning slightly so she faced him better, she moved closer still until her mouth was almost touching his.

He watched her as if mesmerized. Wondering if that was a good sign, she decided she'd take it as positive omen. He wasn't pulling away, or telling her no.

When her lips brushed his, sheer delight flooded through her.

His response was instantaneous, and all she could

have hoped for when he pulled her into his arms and opened his mouth against hers.

Deepening the kiss until she could scarcely think, it was all she'd wanted and more. The sensations that filled her excited. His touch was hot, bringing an exquisite awareness to every inch his fingers grazed. And his hands seemed to be everywhere, in her hair, caressing the length of her back, her arms, even resting briefly against the swell of her tummy.

Sara felt alive. Carefree. Exhilarated. She wound her arms around his neck and brushed his tongue in a dance of delight, exploring his mouth, letting him explore hers.

Blood pounded through her, deafening her with its roar. The sweater became too hot, and together they got it off. His chest begged for attention and her fingers fumbled with his buttons until she could feel the heat of his bare skin, the sheathed steel of his muscles.

When he cupped her breast with his free hand and lightly rubbed the tip, she thought she'd explode with sensations. It was as good as she remembered, *better*. Memory couldn't compete.

She rubbed her fingertips across his chest, remembering the many times she'd done it before, yet feeling as if tonight was the first. His skin was hot, sleek, with a patch of masculine chest hair to tangle her fingers in. When she brushed a copper-colored nipple, she heard his quickly taken breath.

The feminine power that filled her assured her she had forgotten nothing. Not the pleasure she gleaned from his touch, or the pleasure she could provide him with her own loving caresses.

He slipped the top of her dress down, and for a moment time hung suspended. When he pulled her against him, she sighed and wrapped her arms around him, savoring the feel of his chest against her sensitized breasts. Cherishing the feeling of his masculine body cradling hers, his strong arms holding her so gently, his hands stroking her back, sending shivers of awareness coursing through her.

Despite the fact she was eight months pregnant, she felt young and beautiful and desirable.

The baby shifted, and Alec froze. Slowly he ended the kiss, his hand moving from her breast to cover the baby.

She leaned back a bit and looked at him, flushed with passion, wishing she had a clue what he was thinking.

"The most effective chaperone I've ever been around," he said, with a light kiss on her lips. With the same kind of deliberation with which she'd started their kiss, he pulled her dress up, then shifted on the sofa and moved away from her, standing a second later and running the fingers of his unencumbered hand through his hair. He buttoned his shirt.

"I'm going outside for a minute," he said, his back to her.

Left alone, Sara stared at the closed door. Had she made a total idiot of herself? Or was he as affected by the kiss as she'd been? Nothing had prepared her for her reaction. It reminded her of their courting days, when she thought she'd never get enough of Alec.

Once she'd laughed when friends had talked about bells going off, or star bursts, or dazzling rainbows. But not after meeting Alec.

He still had the power to make her world a brighter place.

Tears threatened. She shivered slightly and hugged herself. It wasn't fair. She'd just wanted a husband, a family. She had both, but none of it was unfolding as she'd once dreamed.

Gazing into space, she knew the kaleidoscope of colors and sensations that had flooded showed the full range of passion. Unfortunately passion wasn't enough.

"And that tells you what?" she asked as she got to her feet and grabbed her sweater. Almost running for her room, she knew she was fleeing, but she couldn't be there when Alec returned, as if she were waiting for him to pick up where they left off.

In fact, she now wondered if she could ever face him again! She was not going to start weaving fantasies about a change in their relationship. Not going to imagine he'd miraculously let work slide and concentrate his time on her—not even for a brief vacation.

So he could kiss like no one else. Kisses were fleeting. She wanted more. She needed more.

And not more passion, but a strong, sustained, enduring relationship. She wanted someone she could depend on to share his life with her, not be consumed by a job to the exclusion of his family.

She'd been there, done that and didn't plan to repeat it.

Closing her bedroom door, she leaned against it a moment, then pushed away and began to get ready for bed.

Lying in the dark a little later, she brushed her lips with her fingertips, her heart still pounding. What was she going to do?

Descending the stairs the next morning Sara knew she'd been silly to waste a moment's thought on Alec's reaction. He was glued to the phone again, last night's kisses already forgotten.

She waved a greeting and hurried to the kitchen. Staring in the refrigerator, nothing appealed. She didn't want pancakes again, and she'd had eggs for supper. Deciding to indulge herself, she called the lodge and requested a Jeep. She'd splurge and have a fancy breakfast at the restaurant and see about completing her circuit of the lake by walking home.

When she went to get her purse, she hesitated, knowing the courteous thing to do would be to let Alec know where she was going, but not wishing to interrupt, she rationalized away the urge. They weren't each other's keepers. Chances were he'd never know she was gone.

She stepped out onto the porch just as she heard the Jeep. In no time she sat at one of the large windows in the lodge's restaurant overlooking the lake. She pushed away the thought of how nice it would have been to share breakfast.

After eating, Sara headed for the lake. Her

thoughts were in turmoil. Maybe the walk would help her focus—see things clearly. Such as what Alec wanted, and what they were going to do, and what had been missing from her marriage.

Was it a strong binding love on both sides? She had loved Alec. Had thought he hung the moon. Until he found it necessary to spend more time at work than at home.

She wondered what it would be like if he took time now and then to focus that intensity on her as he had yesterday during their hike. Not once until after they'd slept had she felt he was thinking of work. Maybe a few more outings would show him he could manage a bit more recreation and the world as he knew it wouldn't end.

But she was not on a crusade to save Alec Blackstone. She had her own life to take care of, and plans to make for after her baby was born.

The day was beautiful and the walk easy. This side of the lake was primarily sandy beaches with few trees growing near the water's edge. She waved at fishermen in boats, laughed at the children playing in the two-seater paddle wheels and watched with amazement those who were actually swimming in the cold lake water.

"We'll have to come back here when you're older," she said, rubbing her tummy as the baby stretched and rolled. "You can play in the lake and we can go on the paddle boats together. And explore the caves and have a great vacation."

Smiling dreamily she continued on. It would be nice to have a complete family, mother, father and child. Children. But the only image that rose was that of Alec Blackstone as the father. And Sara firmly squelched it!

Alec was pacing on the porch when the cabin came into view, that cell phone against his ear. How long did the battery last, she wondered. Not that he wasn't charging it every night, but still, she would have thought it would have given out by now.

He saw her and stopped pacing. His eyes watched her as she made her way to the porch.

"I'll call you tomorrow, Teresa. Take the rest of the day off." He clipped the phone shut and leaned one shoulder against the roof support.

"Where have you been?" he asked as Sara mounted the steps.

"For a walk."

He reached out and caught her arm, bringing her closer.

"Did you tell me? I don't remember. I would have followed, but didn't know in which direction you'd gone."

She shook her head. "You were on the phone, remember?"

"You mean when you came down this morning?"

She nodded.

"That was hours ago."

"And how am I supposed to know how long you planned to be on the phone? Usually all day, from what I can tell." His hands on her arms warmed her. His scent filled her. She longed to lean just a bit closer and bury her nose against his chest, relish being this close to him.

"I thought we were going to spend time together, do things together."

"Yesterday showed me how unrealistic that is."

"Didn't you enjoy the hike?"

"Sure, but I wasn't ready to call it a day when you were."

"There—"

She held up her hand. "I do not want to hear about it. If you left that job and went elsewhere, would the city of Boston come to a screeching halt?"

"I'm not leaving to go anywhere else."

"Answer the question, counselor."

"No, of course not."

"Then I suspect it won't come to a screeching halt if you take a few days off." Daringly Sara reached out and took the phone from his pocket. "Starting now, no more phone calls!"

Slowly he drew her closer, until she could feel the warmth from his body, his breath brush across her cheeks.

"If I don't have work, I'll need to occupy my time elsewhere," he said slowly, his other hand capturing the back of her head. "Are you offering to help fill the time?"

Sara stared into his teasing eyes, her breath hitching, her heart racing. The rest of the world seemed to fade away. There were just the two of them, and the pounding excitement that stirred her blood.

"You can put yourself completely in my hands." She'd meant it to be a joke, but her voice came out sultry, sexy. Good grief, was she flirting with him?

"Now that's the best offer I've heard in a while."

He kissed her.

Right out on the front porch where anyone walking by could see!

Kissed her as if they were lovers, deep and sexy and consuming.

And long—as if he had all the time in the world and planned to spend every minute of it with her.

Sara could scarcely think, she could only melt against him and rejoice in the desire that seemed to expand as his mouth again taught hers what pleasure meant.

When she was free, she couldn't move. Her gaze locked with his, seeing the heat in his eyes, the desire, the sheer wanting!

"I suspect your idea of my putting myself in your hands and mine are a bit different," he said, slowly, resting his forehead against hers.

She cleared her throat, wishing he'd stop talking and kiss her again.

"I thought we could go fishing," she said.

Alec laughed and released her. "I haven't been fishing since I was a kid. The best time is early in the morning. Are you up for that?"

So much for passion, she thought wryly. He could turn it off so quickly it must mean nothing to him.

"I can get up early. The boats are at the dock for our use, so we don't have to worry about reserving one. But I don't know about fishing poles." She could be as casual about the situation as he was.

"There are some in the closet. I saw them a couple of days ago. With flies. Unless you want to go the old-fashioned way and dig for worms."

"Yuck, no thanks. I'll stick with the fake lures."

Alec laughed, his eyes never leaving hers. Sara felt a thrill, wondering if he could be falling for her all over again. Or was that mere wishful thinking?

"Where did you go on your walk today?" he asked as the silence stretched out.

"I went to the lodge for breakfast and then walked back. Completed the circle around the lake. And this side is much easier!"

He frowned. "Isn't that a bit far to walk? You've been doing a lot of walking the last few days. Why don't you slow down and take it easy?"

"And do what, watch you talk on the phone?"

He nodded to the phone, still in her hand. "I guess I won't be doing much of that anymore. There's ice cream in the freezer, want some?"

"Only if it's chocolate!"

As they headed inside, Sara wondered what game Alec was playing. She didn't for an instant believe he'd leave his phone in her possession. But for the moment, she felt a heady pleasure in thinking she'd cut off one line of communication. Cut one tie to work. It was a start!

# CHAPTER SEVEN

AFTER dinner they sat on the porch and watched as the sun sank behind the hills. The night was quiet and still. Lights shone through the trees from other cottages. Replete and content, Sara watched as the sky darkened and the first stars appeared.

Alec rose and paced to the edge of the porch. "I feel I ought to be doing something."

"You are, you're resting. Sit down and relax."

"Easy for you to say. You did a lot today, you're probably tired."

"Not especially—I'm just comfy. You worked so you should be tired, too. Sit down. It'll be full dark soon. We can already see some of the stars."

He glanced up briefly, then turned around. "We could go for a walk."

"We could sit here, quietly, and talk," she countered swiftly. "Honestly, it's no wonder you were exhausted when you crashed, you don't cut yourself any slack. There is nothing pressing to be done, nowhere you have to be, just sit and do nothing."

He ran his fingers through his hair and walked over, dropping down into the chair.

Sara would like to run her fingers through his hair and mess it up some more!

"What do you want to talk about? Why is it women always want to talk?" he grumbled.

"Why is it men don't?"

"It's a waste of time."

"How so?" She tried to see him in the growing darkness, but he was merely a silhouette.

"They always want to talk about feelings. A person feels as he feels, talking about it doesn't change anything."

"Sometimes it can explain things, open the door for communications."

He rose again and paced to the stairs. "I feel frustrated, angry I crashed, annoyed as hell that my brother, my doctor, my secretary and everyone else who knows me seems to think I need rest. Outraged you didn't tell me about the baby as soon as you found out. And resentful as hell that you left, and that I still don't understand what makes you tick. So does that foster communications?" he asked sardonically, turning to glare at her.

"You can't let your job alone, it's as if you are obsessed with it. You've made it plain you resent being forced to take vacation. What would foster the beginnings of communications would be to tell me why you can't let go and relax. Why can't you put work aside for three short weeks, recharge and be even more enthusiastic about it when you go back?" Sara returned.

"We had this discussion on the dock the other night. I've agreed to do vacation things with you. And we need to discuss us. I want to know your plans for my baby once it's born."

"One afternoon walk does not a vacation make," she said, ignoring the last part.

"I feel fine. I'm rested."

"Except for dizzy spells and times when your arm aches."

"How did you know my arm aches?"

"I have eyes, counselor. I've seen you cradle it from time to time. And I know broken bones can ache when healing. Rest would help."

"We're back to that."

"Nope. I'm going to bed. If we're getting up early, I want to get a good night's sleep. Or as much as I can with babykins."

"The baby keeps you awake?"

Sara hesitated, then spoke slowly. "Sometimes he or she becomes very active in the night, waking me up and then it's a challenge to get back to sleep."

He leaned against the railing and looked at her, focusing that attention right where she'd once wanted it. Now it made her nervous.

"What exactly are you going to do when the baby arrives?"

"That's one of the things I'm trying to decide on this vacation," Sara said slowly. "I want the best for our baby."

"As do I. Did I figure into your plans at all?"

"Do you want to?"

"You have to ask? Sara, I missed a parent growing up. I don't plan to let any child of mine feel that loss. Yes, I want to be a part of this baby's life!"

"How much? I won't have my baby make plans only to be let down and disappointed when things don't turn out right. You are welcome to come over as often as you like, but we'll only expect you when we see you.''

He frowned. "I would not let the child down.''

"How do I know that? You let *me* down.''

The charged silence stretched on forever.

"I didn't mean to,'' he said softly.

"And you probably wouldn't *mean* to disappoint the baby by making plans and then breaking them when work took precedence. But it would happen. And children grow too fast to let that happen. I want our child to have only happy memories of growing up.''

He was becoming angry again. Was that how she saw the future, him constantly disappointing his son or daughter?

"Give me some credit, Sara, I wouldn't do that.''

Her silence let him know she didn't believe it.

"A visit each week wouldn't be enough. I want to see the baby grow, be a part of teaching him or her about life,'' he said slowly, realizing it was exactly the way he felt. He'd had a part in creating this child, he wanted a strong role in helping it grow to adulthood.

"So what are you suggesting, joint custody? Would you be there enough for that?''

"There are other ways.''

"Like getting back together?''

He stared at her, wondering if that was what he wanted. He hadn't been the one to walk out. Not technically, though he gave nodding acknowledgment to her statement he'd left mentally before she left physically. Could he change? Could he cut back on work and still stay on the fast track?

Sara hesitated near the door and gazed out over the dark expanse in front of her. "Never mind, Alec. I really have it all planned out. My boss has agreed to what I think is a perfect situation. I can work several hours a day and then spend the rest of the time with my baby. There is on-site child care, so I know he or she will get good care while I am working. You and I will work out visitation." She opened the screen. "We can talk about it further another time. Good night."

He was alone on the porch. For a few seconds he could hear her on the stairs, then—nothing. Just the soft wind in the tops of the trees, and the silence of the mountains.

She'd mentioned getting back together. Was it even an option?

Early the next morning, Alec knocked on Sara's bedroom door. He waited a minute then knocked again, louder.

"What? Who is it?" Her sleepy tone flooded him with memories. She took a little while to become awake. They had joked about her not being a morning person. Yet many mornings, he'd awakened to find her watching him. For a moment he was tempted to throw open the door and wake her properly with a kiss. His hand paused over the knob. Did she still wear sheer nighties, or had that only been for him? He knew her hair would be tousled initially, but it was cut so it fell into its short layers with little effort. He ached to see her when she first awoke.

She'd be warm and desirable, he knew. Pushing away the disturbing thoughts, he focused on why he was at the door, dropping his hand to his side.

"Sara, are we on for the fishing expedition?"

"Oh, sure. What time is it?"

"A bit after five. It'll be dawn soon, we want to be on the lake by then."

"I'll be ready in ten minutes."

He could hear activity and slowly, reluctantly, turned from the door. He was dressed and ready to go. He could help her. Pick out something for her to wear, watch her dress.

Her door opened and Sara almost ran into him.

"Oh. Good morning. I'll just be a sec." Bundled in her arms were her clothes. She hurried down the hallway and into the bathroom.

Alec watched her, bemused to discover she slept in a long gown of some soft material that seemed to follow the curves of her body. He took a breath, shocked to discover just seeing her vanish down the hallway had him desiring her. He wanted to forget the fishing trip, take her to bed and make love with his wife all day long!

Frowning, he went downstairs to the kitchen and tried to occupy himself by making coffee. Before long the fragrant aroma filled the air. Taking time to find the herbal tea she drank, he prepared her a cup.

"Ah, a man after my own heart," Sara said. She entered and made a beeline to the mug he held out. "I know I said I wanted to go fishing, but think I need a bit more time to psych myself up for this early rising. I am on vacation!''

He leaned against the counter and watched her bustle around. She sipped the hot beverage and gave a blissful smile. Quickly she prepared bagels and cream cheese and handed him one.

''This will hold us. Will we be out long enough to need a lunch?'' she asked, taking another sip of tea.

''No, we'll come back by then. Ready?'' Alec felt irritated with the feelings he was experiencing. It seemed right to share chores in the kitchen. They worked well together—but he wanted to share more than chores. He wanted to be back in Sara's bed!

''I'm ready,'' she said as she swallowed another bite of bagel. ''I can take this with me and finish by the time we reach the boat.''

The morning was cool, the sun just rising above the hills to the east. The sky was already changing color. The air was hushed as they took the pine needle strewn path to the lake. None of their neighbors seemed awake.

Alec carried the fishing gear while Sara finished eating her bagel.

There were two boats moored at the dock. Alec chose one and dropped down into it, steadying himself as it rocked a bit. He placed the fishing poles to the side and reached up to help Sara in.

He reached for her waist, encountering the swell of baby. She laughed and the sound warmed him. He liked her laughter. Something else he'd missed over the past months.

"I feel like a sausage," she said as she rested her hands on his shoulders and lightly stepped down into the boat. It rocked wildly and he held her tightly.

"Whoa, don't capsize us."

"I wouldn't dare. That water is freezing." Sitting gingerly on one of the bench seats, she looked up brightly. "This is a great idea."

Alec stepped to the stern and checked the small trolling motor. Seeing the gas tank was full, he pulled the cord and it started immediately. The soft hum of the motor sounded loud in the early-morning stillness.

"We're going to wake everyone up," Sara said, turning to watch him cast off and guide the little boat away from the dock.

"It's not that noisy. None of the boats on the lake woke you on other mornings, did they?"

She looked around. There were at least a half-dozen boats scattered around the glassy surface. She had heard none of them.

By the time they stopped, and Alec cut the motor to allow them to drift slowly, the sun had risen. Some of the chill abated and he settled back.

"I've never been fishing before, so you have to show me what to do," Sara said, shifting, rocking the boat. "Oops. How do we move around?"

"We don't. Hand me that blue box, it has the flies. I'll get you going."

A few minutes later both had lines in the water— on opposite sides of the boat. Sara looked relaxed, blissfully gazing over the water, anticipation evident. Alec was amused. Obviously she expected to land a fish instantly. As the minutes ticked by, he watched her. Her anticipation waned as frustration mounted.

She glanced at him, frowned.

"What's funny?"

"Nothing."

Narrowing her eyes, she glared at him. "You're definitely amused."

He nodded.

"Why?"

"You look as if you expect the fish to just jump in the boat. Fishing is a slow, longtime process. Relaxing, remember?"

"I don't feel relaxed. I'm afraid the boat's going to tip over if I don't keep a constant balance. Or I'll drop the pole, or the fish will yank it out of my hand. And one thing I don't think we took into consideration was the frequency with which pregnant women need a rest room!"

His lips twitched. So much for a relaxing morning on the lake.

"Should I head for home now?"

She shook her head, now glaring at the fishing pole and the line. "No, I'm good for a while yet. But I thought we'd have a fish by now. I thought we could have a fish fry today like the Simpsons did. Return their hospitality so to speak."

"Relax. Given enough time, we'll probably catch as many as Mr. Simpson did."

"Oh great, the workaholic himself is telling me to relax?"

Alec laughed aloud at her disgruntled tone. When she looked at him, her eyes sparkled and she grinned.

Suddenly he no longer felt like laughing. He wanted to pull her into his arms and kiss her again. Feel that warm weight of her body, the new shapes and contours he was growing to know. Wanted to taste her mouth, breathe in her special scent. Wanted that feeling of connection he felt when they embraced.

Frowning at his thoughts, he turned away just as he felt a tug on his line. Setting the hook, he let the fish play a bit before reeling him in.

Sara was so excited he was afraid she would capsize them. "Sit still," he said, pulling a bit more on the rod, swiftly turning the reel.

"But you have a fish! Get it! I want to see."

"Pay attention to your pole. You could get one soon and lose the rod if you aren't paying attention," Alec warned.

Just then she gave a yelp. "I have a fish! I have a fish!" She almost bounced on the seat.

The boat rocked again and he just knew he was going to end up in the water—cast not withstanding.

His fish came out of the water, gleaming in the sun. He swung it into the boat.

"*Eech*, don't let it touch me," Sara screamed, moving as far from the floundering fish as she could. Her own pole was forgotten momentarily as she stared at Alec's fish. She moved her feet to the other side of the bench and looked around. "What are you going to put it in? You can't just leave it at the bottom of the boat!"

"We have a creel, that's the big brown wicker container in the bow. Hand it back."

Gingerly she reached for it and tossed it to him.

"How's your fish?" he asked as he deftly un-hooked his catch and dropped it into the creel.

"Oh, I don't know!" Sara turned back to her rod and began to reel it in. In only a moment she had a fish dangling from the end, swinging back and forth.

"Bring it into the boat," Alec said, almost laughing at the perplexed look on her face. Fishing with Sara was nothing like fishing with Wyatt had been.

She turned, and the fish almost whacked him in the face. He ducked, then reached up and nabbed the dangling creature. In only a second, he had it free and in the creel.

"I need to go back," Sara said, placing her rod in the boat and turning to face the bow.

"Tired of fishing already?"

She shook her head. "But I think I need to do my fishing from the dock. I need to go back, Alec, and right now."

Alec took them back and had barely nudged the dock before Sara leaped up and hopped onto the wooden pier.

"I'll be back in a minute," she said and almost ran up the path. He sat in the boat, watching her.

Now what? Was that the end of their fishing expedition? He looked at his watch—it was still early. Looking over the lake, he noticed more boats.

Suddenly he realized he wanted to go back out. Wanted to laze away the morning bobbing on the water, listening to Sara talk, watching her fish. Teresa would be arriving at work soon, but for once the urgent need to check in was missing.

Sara was right, the legal system of Boston would

not come to a halt because he wasn't there. He'd check in later, maybe when Sara napped. She'd never know.

Not that it mattered if she knew or not. Yet somehow he didn't want to disappoint her.

He watched the path. How long would she be?

By lunchtime Sara was tired and certain she didn't want to go fishing again anytime soon. There were aspects she liked, like drifting along on the water, Alec's biting sense of humor, the idyllic setting.

But there were an equal number of discomforting things: touching the fish when taking them off the hook, the constant caution needed to make sure she didn't capsize the boat, the trips back to the dock so she could meet her body's needs.

Alec never complained, he took her back each time she requested it. Even with his cast, he handled the boat as if he'd been doing it all his life.

She'd been surprised after that first return to find him at the dock waiting for her. Her heart did that funny little flip and settled down to beating faster than normal. Or normal when away from Alec. She was beginning to think that rapid pace was her standard whenever in his proximity. Surely she should be over that reaction by now.

She offered to stay on the dock, but he insisted he didn't want to fish alone.

Of course, she'd done more than her fair share of talking. He'd ask a question and she'd talk for twenty minutes. No wonder he was so terrific as an attorney; getting witnesses to talk had to be a piece of cake for him. She wondered if she could see him in action one day. Odd she'd never found the time before. Maybe Elizabeth would know when he was in court and she could slip into the back and listen to him.

Not that she wanted to think that far ahead. Today was enough. They'd had a great morning.

"I'm impressed," she said as he tied up the boat.

"With my boating skills?" he asked, handing up the rods, and the heavy creel after she clambered onto the dock. He lightly jumped up beside her.

"Okay, that, too, but the fact you never mentioned your caseload a single time all morning."

"I thought about it every time you ran up to the cabin," he said, tapping her on the chin with his finger. "And I'm going down to the main lodge while you take your nap."

"So much for thinking you were reformed," she said in mock distress as they turned and began walking to the cottage. The Simpsons came down the path, stopping to greet them.

"We're on our way to do some fishing—hope you didn't catch all the fish," Paul Simpson said.

"I thought you had to get an early start for fishing," Sara said, turning her suspicious gaze on Alec. "At least that's what I was told."

Paul laughed. "That works, too, but we're on vacation and didn't want to get up early. They may not bite as much now, but being together is what we're after, not necessarily fish."

"Good luck," she said as the older couple continued toward the dock.

"They're nice, aren't they?" she said watching them wistfully.

"I thought we established that after dinner the other night. They are nice. They are in love. They have a happy marriage. And they most likely are the exception that proves the rule," Alec said as they entered the shady area. The coolness felt good after the warmth of the sun.

"Cynic."

"Realist."

"Wyatt and Elizabeth are in love and have a happy marriage."

"And it's lasted two years so far. Is that some kind of record?"

She heard the teasing in his tone, but refused to rise to the bait. It hurt too much in light of the fact their marriage had not reached the two-year mark. Shrugging she changed the subject.

"So are you going to clean these fish? Or at least show me how?"

"I'll clean them."

"I'd watch, except I'm really sleepy."

"It's all this fresh air and sunshine."

"Maybe." Or maybe it was because she had trouble falling asleep last night after their discussion about the baby. She longed for the perfect family and instead had come to the point of considering a divorce from her husband.

Not that she'd thought about that in days. She wasn't thinking about staying married, was she?

"I wish we'd caught enough to invite the others over," she said to take her mind off her thoughts.

"Maybe tomorrow."

"Maybe not. I don't want to get up at the crack of dawn two days in a row."

"Then we can go hiking tomorrow up to the meadow and explore those caves."

"Sounds like a great plan. You'll love them. You can recapture your childhood. I'll play Wyatt's part as a pirate."

Alec dropped his arm across her shoulders. "Somehow it won't be the same thing. Not that I'm complaining, understand."

"I'll make a great pirate."

"I think you'd make a better captive. The beautiful lady captured for a ransom."

"Who would ransom me?"

"Ah, but if I don't get the ransom, I get to have my wicked way with you." He twirled an imaginary mustache.

Sara laughed, though her heart pounded at the thought of Alec having his way with her. Of his mouth against hers, his hard body merged with hers.

She could hardly speak as the vision danced before her eyes, of her in Alec's embrace. Of his mouth pressed against hers, of his hands roaming like a pirate over every inch of her. Inflaming her, captivating her, enchanting her.

Thoughts of sleeping fled. Fatigue vanished. Suddenly her blood was rushing through her, her skin tingled in awareness and excitement.

It was madness. Not midsummer's madness, but vacation insanity all the same. They had tried once and it hadn't worked. His hopes were vastly different from hers, his goals and dreams diametrically opposed to hers.

Only the tenuous strand of physical compatibility had held them together. She would be foolish to think anything had changed.

When they reached the cottage, Alec went straight to the kitchen, cleaning the fish, wrapping them and stowing them in the refrigerator. Sara watched for a while, but the smell began to make her feel sick. She wished he'd say something or do something to show he was as aware of her as she was of him.

So much for mutual feelings, she thought as she trekked up the steps to take her daily nap. Pulling over a light cover, she turned on her side, tried to get comfortable, to relax. Tried to talk some sense into herself.

But she was disappointed he so easily ignored the fun morning they'd shared. Truly there was no hope for workaholics like Alec. No matter what, work came first. She'd learned that once, why couldn't she hold that thought?

Sara slept fitfully, waking late in the afternoon, not feeling refreshed. Alone in the cottage, she took her time in a warm shower, washing her hair. It took only minutes for the short style to dry, and she spent the time on the porch, enjoying the serenity of the late afternoon.

She began to wonder when Alec would return. Then frowned when she realized what she was doing. She was self-sufficient. She didn't need him to complete her vacation. She had books to read, magazines to glance through, and some serious thinking to do.

But, instead, she remained on the porch, watching the road, listening for the sound of a Jeep, daydreaming the afternoon away.

Checking her watch some time later, she realized it would soon be seven and she was getting hungry. She had spent too many nights in the past waiting in vain for Alec to return home at a reasonable hour.

Grilling the fish fillets, she prepared a salad and corn bread. When dinner was ready, she set the table and sat alone while she ate. The view from the window was delightful, the sun still a fiery ball in the sky, sinking behind the tall trees.

The prick of loneliness was to be expected, she comforted herself. She had spent a lot of time with Alec over the past few days, now alone once more she missed him. But just as a companion, someone to talk with during dinner, she assured herself.

Why did she feel like she was lying?

Covering his plate, she put it away. He could warm it up when he returned—if he hadn't already eaten at the lodge.


Alec opened the door and braced himself for recriminations and complaints.

The living room was empty. Two lamps provided soft illumination. There was a lingering hint of cooked fish in the air. His mouth watered. Walking to the kitchen, he pushed open the door. It was dark and empty.

Listening, he heard nothing. Had Sara gone out?

He let the door close and carried his briefcase to the sofa. Laying it down, he ignored the tinge of disappointment. He'd stayed longer than he'd anticipated at the guest office. He fully expected Sara to have berated him, complain she'd prepared dinner and he'd missed it. Get huffy and annoyed he'd put work ahead of relaxation.

Not that she'd care, but he had a valid reason. A compelling reason.

He heard a sound from the bathroom. Mounting the stairs swiftly, he walked down the short hall. The door was shut, but he could hear humming behind it.

Alec knocked lightly. "Sara?"

"Hi, Alec." Her voice sounded bright and cheery. "Did you need the bathroom? I can be out in a few minutes."

"No, I just got home and wondered where you were."

"I'm taking a bubble bath."

He leaned his forehead against the door, closing his eyes as he imagined her skin rosy and glowing and strategically covered with bubbles. He'd like to wipe his hands over that slick, heated skin, push aside the bubbles and—

"—so you'll have to heat it, but it still should be good."

"What?"

"Dinner." She raised her voice. "In the refrigerator. Heat it up and it'll be good. Unless you already ate."

"No. Did you cook the fish?"

"Yes. And it turned out delicious! Go eat."

The meal was as delicious as she'd promised. Sara had always been a talented cook. He wished he had been there when she first cooked it. He could imagine her pride in eating the catch of the day.

When he heard the door open upstairs, he went on alert. Would she come down, or was she relaxed and ready for bed? He finished the meal and placed the empty plate on the end table, all the while watching the stairs.

# CHAPTER EIGHT

SARA felt totally relaxed and in a great mood. She debated going to bed, but it was still early, and she knew she wouldn't sleep, not after her fitful dozing that afternoon. Studying her reflection in the mirror, she decided she looked respectable enough to visit with Alec before bed. The long robe flowed around her, keeping the evening mountain chill at bay, and looked flattering with its deep rose color. Her hair was damp around the edges, but would dry soon.

No makeup, she decided laying down the lipstick. She certainly didn't want Alec to get the wrong impression.

Taking a breath, she headed downstairs.

"Dinner was wonderful," he said as she reached the bottom of the steps. He rose from the chair and gestured to the sofa.

It was safer to keep her distance, she thought, crossing to a matching armchair. "Glad you liked it. It was really good when first done. Did it heat up well?"

"Better than I had a right to expect. I'm sorry I'm late getting back."

She shrugged. "It's your vacation, spend it as you wish." Proud of the casualness of her tone, Sara looked at the fireplace, wishing they had built a small fire. Flickering flames would give her something to look at. Instead she wanted to look at Alec. And dared not indulge herself.

"Something unexpected came up."

"Mmm."

"Remember I told you I'm going to trial with a case when I return?"

She nodded, facing him.

"We found an unexpected witness, which throws a monkey wrench in the whole works. I'm trying to coordinate the change in strategy from here. I had to talk with the legal assistant, with the opposing attorney and with the arresting officer."

"Does it weaken your case?" she asked, flattered he'd talk about his work with her. He so rarely had done so before.

"It could." Alec talked at some length about the initial strategy and the new plans undertaken. Then he broke off.

"I'm sorry, this must be boring for you."

"No. I'm fascinated. I thought earlier that I missed something by never coming to see you in action. I wish I had. Maybe I'll stop by the court one day and watch."

She almost laughed at his expression. He was obviously taken aback.

"I like the law, but it can get tedious sometimes," he said.

"You make it sound exciting and worthwhile. I bet you're great in the courtroom."

He shrugged. "Tell me when you're coming and I'll make sure you have a front row seat."

"I might just do that."

They fell silent, their eyes never moving from each other. Sara began to feel that fluttering inside. Her skin heated and awareness shimmered. The baby moved and broke the spell. What was she doing? Considering a divorce, she had no business flirting with Alec just to pass the time. Yet neither had really brought up the dreaded "D" word. And now was not the time.

"I guess I'll go up," she said, standing. She needed some space, to gain some perspective. Coming downstairs had her dreaming things that could never be. She needed to get over the notion he found her attractive. She was eight months pregnant, for heaven's sake! Even a man besotted wouldn't find a woman all that attractive at this stage. And Alec had never struck her as besotted even on their best day together.

"Tomorrow night, would you have dinner with me at the lodge? I booked a table. They have a nice combo, I heard it tonight from the hall when passing the restaurant. We could stay for the dancing."

Sara wanted to say yes. The thought almost made her giddy. But something held her back. It wasn't a date, precisely, just roommates sharing a meal. And maybe a dance or two.

"I don't know—"

"Say yes. You have to eat, might as well let someone else do the cooking for one night."

"Okay, then. Yes, thank you." Well that put paid to any thoughts of romantic entanglements. How prosaic could he get? They both had to eat, why not eat at the lodge?

"Good night." She passed him on the way to the stairs and for one moment thought he'd reach out and—

"Good night, Sara."

The next morning when Sara entered the kitchen, Alec was at the table, a pile of what looked like thick, tangled string in front of him. The delicious aroma of coffee filled the air.

He glanced up. "I made coffee."

"Smells good. Wish I could have some. What in the world is that?"

"A hammock. James dropped by a few minutes ago. He and Hilary are heading home today. They got the hammock from the lodge the first day, said it's great for loafing in the shade."

"I haven't been in a hammock for years," she said as she filled the teakettle. Taking a seat at the table while she waited for the water to heat, she touched the soft strands. "Can you put it up?"

"Yes, James showed me where the hooks are." Alec looked up. "It's a double."

"Oh."

"I thought I'd mention that in case you had delusions of resting in solitary isolation this afternoon."

She waved her hand dismissingly. "Not to worry, you'll be at the office at the lodge. I'll have it all to myself."

"Don't bet the farm on it, lady. I have a hankering to test a hammock. My grandparents had one. Wyatt and I used to fight over who got it until they worked out some schedule.''

''We could do that, I suppose,'' she said.

''Work out a schedule?''

Nodding, Sara chanced a glance. The dancing amusement in his eyes was mesmerizing. She smiled, raising her eyebrows. ''No?''

''Not a chance, sweetheart. Unless you go from nine to midnight.''

''While you take the one to three in the afternoon?''

''Sounds fair.''

''Ha, in your dreams, Blackstone. I get first dibs, I'm the pregnant one.''

''And in all good conscience, I couldn't leave you and the baby alone in this contraption. What if you had difficulty getting up? We know how frequently you need to use the facilities.''

''A low blow!''

''We can try it out after lunch.''

''Maybe.'' The thought of the two of them in the hammock, lying together, almost made her forget breakfast. Grasping it as an excuse to leave the table, Sara went to the refrigerator and began pulling out eggs, spinach and cheese. She'd make an omelet, and not think about sharing a hammock!

''So what do you want to do this morning?'' Alec asked, leaning back to watch her work.

Aware of his eyes on her, she felt nervous. Self-conscious. ''I don't know. Don't you have things to do?''

''Not today. I've put in motion the investigations

I need for the trial, now I'm delegating and letting others handle the preliminary work.''

Sara turned in amazement. ''Did I hear you right? You're going to delegate?''

He nodded. ''So how about that paddle wheel? We managed the rowboat fine, we're ready.''

''Are you sure about this?'' Sara asked an hour later as they stood on the dock studying the flimsy-looking paddle boat. Two seats were side by side, pedals on the floor, which propelled the paddles in the rear. One set for each seat.

Alec scanned the lake. ''I've seen people using these all week. None have capsized.''

''Getting dumped wouldn't be my idea of fun,'' she said hesitantly. Tossing her head, she grinned. ''Let's do it.''

Carefully stepping in, she took the seat farthest from the dock. A moment later the craft bobbed as Alec stepped in and sat beside her.

It was a close fit. His hip pressed against hers, his thigh touched hers. His shoulders seemed too big. She held her breath. This was never going to work.

''Okay, we're on our own,'' he said as he tossed the rope onto the dock. Slowly she began to pedal. He shifted, the boat swayed from side to side.

''Watch it!'' she squealed, feeling a splash of water.

Draping his arm across her shoulder, he settled in. ''It's too crowded—I think these were designed with smaller people in mind.''

''Still, it's fun.'' Slowly they moved away from

the dock. Sunshine glinted on the water, the tall spruce and pines lining the lake were silhouetted against a pristine blue sky. A light breeze danced across the surface, reducing the sun's intensity.

When Alec pedaled faster, the craft went in circles. Sara laughed and tried to keep up, to make her paddle go as fast to straighten out their direction.

The day was perfect, she thought as they began to work in tandem. She laughed at Alec's nonsense, and secretly enjoyed the feel of his body against hers, his arm across her shoulders, his leg bumping hers as they paddled, sometimes furiously, sometimes languidly.

"Wyatt and Elizabeth missed a great vacation," she said as they turned and began to head for the dock some time later.

"No yearnings for Europe?"

"No, this is more fun. I speak the language, understand the money and don't have to be packing my bags and moving on every other day. I wish I had even more time. It seems as if the days are flying by."

"We still have a few days left."

She nodded. The one cloud on the horizon was knowing this would all come to an end soon. Would she ever see Alec once they parted? Would he truly be interested in seeing her and their baby or would they each become caught up in their own lives and never find the time? It made her sad to think of it.

"Are you all right?" he asked.

"Sure." She shook off her mood and smiled. "This is so much fun. I knew it would be."

When he didn't respond, she turned at looked at him. His gaze was fixed on her.

"Are you having fun?" she asked softly.

"Yes, Sara, I'm having fun."

Slowly he leaned closer, his arm tightening on her shoulders. When his lips touched hers, she closed her eyes to better relish the enchanting sensations. They stopped pedaling, and the kiss went on and on.

Sara knew she never wanted it to stop.

Alec pulled back, his eyes opening, then closing. "Either you are extraordinary at kicking my senses crazy, or I'm having another one of those dammed dizzy attacks!" He gingerly sat back, holding on to Sara like a lifeline.

"I'd love to take credit but I don't think so," she said. "Do you have any medicine on you?"

"No, I haven't had a problem in a couple of days. I thought I was finally over them."

"Can you pedal? We have to get you back to the dock."

Gritting his teeth, he opened his eyes a slit and nodded. Slowly they pedaled the boat. As they drew closer, she could see the strain in his face. Reaching the dock wouldn't solve all their problems, they still had to walk to the cabin.

"We're almost there. Are you going to be able to get out? Should I run up to get Mr. Simpson to help?" she asked as they drew near the dock.

"I don't need help."

Typical male reaction, she thought. But if she didn't think he could cope, she'd stuff his reaction and go for help anyway!

Alec proved he could manage, stepping from the boat while she held it steady. In two seconds she tied it up and stood on the dock beside him.

Taking his arm, she slowly pointed him in the direction of the path.

"I can manage," he said.

"I know, I'm just here in case you need me."

His smile was sardonic. "And what can you do if I fall, cushion me?"

"You're not going to fall. Come on, once we get back to the cottage you can lie down and take those pills."

"I hate this!" he ground out.

"I'm sure you do." Anything that slowed him down had to be despised. Alec liked to be in charge, in control. Yet he was only human, and needed to let his body recover at its own rate.

He walked as if drunk, weaving and staggering once or twice despite his arm draped around Sara's shoulder. She was glad she was with him. He remained silent on the short walk to the cabin, but she suspected he resented needing her help. And heaven help him if he had an attack at the lodge. He'd remain forever in the guest services office rather than ask for assistance.

Leaving him on the sofa when they reached the cabin, Sara ran lightly up the stairs to his room to find the pills. Satisfied a few minutes later that he would recover with some rest, Sara headed for the kitchen. She'd prepare a light lunch and see if Alec felt like eating. She was ravenous after the morning on the boat, and her legs were pleasantly tired from all the paddling.

Alec insisted on sitting at the table for lunch. Worried, Sara watched him closely as he ate, until he snapped at her.

"I'm fine. I don't need a nursemaid."

"What you probably need is more rest. You can have first turn on the hammock."

"I don't need first turn. You're the one who takes naps in the afternoons, you take it."

"I can lie down later, or if I get tired, I can use my bed."

He shook his head impatiently, then stopped, looking at her with narrowed eyes. "It's a double."

"And we'd get a lot of rest sharing, I'm sure." She hadn't forgotten a single one of their kisses.

What would it be like to lie down and sleep beside Alec again? Would he put his arm around her like they used to sleep? Snuggle close? Or turn his back and snore?

She almost giggled at that scenario. He'd never snored. He'd be much more likely to draw her into his arms and kiss her, let his hands roam over the changed contours of her body—

The thoughts jumbled in her head and she tried to ignore them. He was still recovering from a serious accident, and she did get tired in the afternoon. Splurging on naps was the height of luxury. After the baby was born and she returned to work, there'd be no more napping.

"Okay, I guess," she said slowly. "But only if we rest."

"What else would we do?"

She almost told him, but the amusement dancing in his eyes let her know he knew exactly what she meant. Firmly closing her mouth, she concentrated on her food. After a minute, she realized he had not agreed to the rest only edict. Responding with a question was a neat ploy. Should she make him promise?

That would make it seem a bigger deal than it was. She'd take her chances. Anticipation hummed.

They strung up the hammock between the two trees where James had showed Alec. It was a wide, lacy net hammock and once in position rested several feet above the ground. Sara eyed it dubiously.

"I don't know."

"I'll go first." He eased back on the woven surface, sitting in the middle, then leaned back and lifted his legs. Scooting slowly, carefully, to one side, he patted the place beside him as the hammock swayed gently.

The surface was big. There was room enough for both with space on either side. Dappled shade sheltered them and the scent of pine wafted in the warm afternoon air.

Nothing ventured, Sara thought as she moved to sit gingerly on the edge.

"Not so close to the edge, scoot back," Alec warned.

But she wasn't as agile as she normally was and plopped on the very edge, throwing the hammock off balance, sliding down on the ground with a thump and dumping Alec practically on top of her.

Surprised, she stared at his stunned expression, then burst out laughing.

"Think that's funny, do you?" he asked, pushing her gently back on the pine needles and coming down to kiss her senseless.

Sara reached up and encircled his neck with her arms, pulling him off balance until he sprawled half across her and half on the ground. She opened her mouth and kissed him back with all the pent-up desire she possessed.

Suddenly she knew why the day was perfect— Alec was with her. She was falling in love with him all over again. Just being with him made everything brighter, more enjoyable.

Shocked, she tried to pull back, but he wasn't ready. His tongue danced against hers, sending shimmering excitement tingling throughout her body. His hard chest pressed against her. She wished she could run her hands over his muscles, feel the heat of his skin, know she made him feel some of the raw power his kiss made her feel.

When he shifted slightly, she opened her eyes, and gazed deeply into his. Neither spoke, but words weren't necessary. She wanted to capture the moment, hold on to it, keep it safe from all outside influences. Why couldn't they stay in a world of two forever?

"Are you all right?" he asked.

She nodded, slowly pulling her hands away. "I'm sorry you fell. It didn't jar your arm did it?"

He shook his head. "There's a technique to hammocks." He rose in one lithe motion, and reached down to pull her up. "When you sit, make sure you are far enough back from the edge that you don't throw off the center of gravity."

She nodded, wondering how he could talk. Her heart raced, her skin tingled, blood rushed through her at warp speed, and the heat that enveloped her matched that of the sun. And he talked as if nothing had happened. Did he kiss everyone he knew that way?

Then she noticed his breathing was almost as rapid as hers. Satisfaction swept through her. He might look impervious, but that kiss had disturbed him, too. There was some justice in the world after all!

Following the firm instructions, Sara managed to get on the hammock without incident. She lay next to Alec and gazed up at the sky through the trees. She was far too aware of the man next to her to feel sleepy. How was she supposed to get any rest in his proximity?

Yet, in only a few moments her eyes closed and she drifted off.

When Sara awoke, her head was pillowed on Alec's shoulder, one arm thrown across his chest. Her stomach rested against his. His arm held her loosely. She lay still, trying to figure out how she'd moved into this position. His scent mingled with that of the pines. The sweet fragrance of distant flowers drifted on the breeze. The slow rise and fall of his chest attested to the fact he was sound asleep.

Afraid to move for fear of waking him, or falling off, she relaxed. It had been a long time since they'd been like this. It felt good. Right.

Wishing to treasure the moment, she tried to imprint every detail in her mind. She'd taken their time together for granted before. Now that they didn't have a future together, she knew she had to capture every fleeting moment. Savor each one. Treasure them. She didn't want to repeat the mistakes she'd made the first time around. Expecting a bright future wasn't in the cards.

That fact apparently didn't stop her from loving him. Or from admiring his strength, his dedication. And didn't stop her from wishing for the moon. Reality would intrude all too soon. For this afternoon, and this evening, she'd enjoy herself.

When they parted, she'd have to cope once again with the problem of falling in love with a man who could never fully love in return. But she didn't have to deal with that today.

The baby moved, bumping against Alec. Sara might not have a future with the man beside her, but she had her baby. And she'd make sure to give her child the best family life she could—even if it was just the two of them. She would teach her son or daughter to love wholeheartedly. And take chances.

"Are you awake?" he asked, startling her. Thank goodness he couldn't read minds.

She nodded, rubbing her cheek against his shoulder, reluctant to move, to end this special time.

"How do you feel? No dizziness?" she asked.

"None."

The minutes stretched out. Sara smiled slightly. Neither moved. Was he enjoying this time together as much as she? Did he have similar regrets their marriage hadn't worked?

Finally Alec shifted slightly, and Sara pushed up as much as she could against the ever shifting hammock.

"Still up for dinner and dancing tonight?" he asked.

"Wouldn't you rather stay home? I mean, what if you have another dizzy spell?"

"I've already made the reservation. The attacks are growing farther and farther apart. I doubt I'll have another one tonight."

"Okay, then, I'd love to go to dinner."

The lodge seemed bustling and crowded after the slow, quiet pace of the cabin that Sara had enjoyed over the past few days. While not full, more than half the tables in the restaurant were occupied. A combo played softly. The food was delicious, and Alec continued to fascinate her. They exchanged stories of other vacations. It seemed sad she had so many to relate while he had only a few from his childhood.

"You need to make time for vacations more often," she said.

He rubbed his chin and nodded slowly, his gaze moving around the room, ending up on her. "This has turned out better than I expected. Maybe it's the company I'm keeping."

"Vacations are more fun shared," Sara agreed, glowing from the comment.

By the time other couples began to dance, they had finished dinner.

"Care to try?" he asked, nodding to the dance floor.

"Sure do."

"We can have dessert later."

"Nothing for me, I'm full."

He rose and she was struck again at how handsome he looked in the dark sports coat, white shirt and pants. She wore a sundress that had been the most dressy piece of clothing she'd brought. Her sandals were flat, but better for her than high heels would have been, given her altered center of gravity.

She moved into his arms as if they'd danced together many times before. Odd, she couldn't remember but one night they'd gone dancing before. Tonight was heavenly. His cast ignored, she snuggled closer and gave herself up to the rhythm of the music and the fantasy of a future that skipped just out of reach.

"You never told me where you learned to dance so well?" Sara asked as he moved her around the floor in intricate patterns. "Here I thought you were a diehard attorney, never stepping a foot outside a law library."

He smiled into her eyes. Her heart skipped a beat. Her knees grew weak and it was all she could do to miss his toes. Wouldn't that go over great, stumbling around like a love-struck teenager!

"I learned in college. I thought it might come in handy to make points with the boss's wife at functions."

"Always an eye to the main chance, huh?" she teased.

"Isn't that the way to get ahead?"

"And what are you getting ahead for?"

He twirled them around, then settled in a slower rhythm as the music softened, slowed.

"What do you mean? That's the great American dream, getting ahead."

"But what for? What will you do when you are ahead? And when will that be? When you're ninety—too old to enjoy anything? Or next year, or when you're a millionaire? When does it end?"

He didn't respond immediately. Finally he shrugged, "I'll know it when I see it."

"I think it's become habit. And you won't ever stop."

"Why should I? I like what I do."

"It's sort of one-sided, isn't it? I mean, you work all the time—even here."

The music ended and he released her. "I think on this issue, we're going to have to agree to disagree."

She nodded, feeling sad that he seemed to be missing some of the joys in life.

Her comment annoyed Alec. He had things going just the way he liked them. For the most part.

As they walked back to the table, he watched her. Holding her head proudly, moving with such grace, he was struck with how much he'd enjoyed the time at the resort.

No longer railing against fate, he'd accepted the downtime and given his staff a bit more autonomy.

Which might prove to be a good move. Time would tell.

And time was running out on his enforced vacation. He had an appointment with the doctor in Boston in three more days. Once he left the resort, he didn't plan to return. If the doctor continued to harp on more time off, he'd spend it at his apartment.

Suddenly he realized the thought held no appeal. There'd be no bright-eyed enthusiastic woman there to share the hours. No lake to walk beside, or gaze at from a porch. No fish to catch.

"I changed my mind," Sara said as he held her chair for her. "I might have some of that chocolate concoction that I saw when we walked by that couple." She nodded at a nearby table.

He flagged a waiter and gave the order.

"I shouldn't," she said, with a dreamy look on her face. For a moment Alec felt almost jealous of a stupid piece of cake. He wished Sara would look at him that way—just once more.

"But I do so love chocolate!" She looked at him. "Want to share?"

"Yes." He wanted some of her cake, and some of her lightness and happiness. For the first time in years, work faded in importance.

Impatiently Alec waited for the dessert, ate his half in a couple of bites and as soon as Sara finished, whisked her onto the dance floor again. He liked holding her in his arms, moving with her to the tempo of the music. Maybe it was time to take this vacation to the next level. She was receptive to his kisses. More than receptive, her mouth was a delight.

Her own spark of passion ignited his every time they touched.

It was late when he noticed how tired she looked. "Ready to go home?" he asked.

She nodded. "I'm really tired. Despite the nap, I think all that exercise on the water and the dancing has done me in."

In only moments they were in one of the courtesy Jeeps, being driven through the darkness, the headlights the only source of illumination in addition to the stars overhead.

Alec tipped the driver, and took Sara's hand when they climbed the steps to the porch. The darkness enveloped them when the Jeep turned the bend and was lost from view. For a moment Alec remembered that first morning. Nothing had gone as he'd anticipated. Too bad he couldn't have foreseen the future.

"I'll have a light on in a sec," he said, opening the door.

"I'm going up," she said. "I had a great time tonight. Thanks."

Staying by the end table he nodded. She still looked exhausted. Not the most auspicious time to explore the possibility of more intimacy. He'd wait. They still had three more days before he had to leave.

"Good night."

He watched her climb the stairs, then checked his watch. It was too late to go back to the lodge to use their guest office. And too late to call his secretary even if he had his cell phone.

Maybe he'd read. He still had those adventure books Wyatt had optimistically given him. Feeling restless, Alec went to his bedroom and changed into jeans then dug out one of the books. He heard nothing from Sara's room. Was she already asleep?

Crossing the hall, he tapped gently on her door. Then turned the knob. Opening it slightly, he saw her lying in bed, already fast asleep.

She slept on her side, one hand beneath her cheek as she had at their picnic. It reminded him of that afternoon when he'd awoken in the hammock with her head on his shoulder. He should have tightened his arm and brought her across to rest fully on his chest. Should have kissed her breathless and seen where that would have taken them.

Now he had to wait. And Alec didn't like to wait.

Sara felt out of sorts when she awoke the next morning. The sound of rain on the roof almost had her groaning. Great, she felt cranky and it was going to be a rainy day! No chance to go for a walk to clear her mind. What would she and Alec do, cooped up in the cabin all day?

She'd gone immediately to sleep upon arriving home last night. But around three she'd woken and found it almost impossible to fall back asleep. Her thoughts had centered on Alec, and her growing feelings. How could she have been so dumb as to fall for him when he continued to show the same tendencies as before to put work before her.

It was her own fault. Foolish her.

When Sara wandered downstairs some time later, she knew the house was empty. Glancing out the window, she watched the rain for a few minutes. Everything looked gray and dreary and cold. Shivering slightly, she went to the kitchen to prepare something to eat.

The note was propped next to the teakettle. His handwriting was bold, strong. Just like the man.

She tossed the note back on the counter. No surprise, he'd gone to the lodge to check in at work. Of course with the unexpected change in his pending case, he probably did need to keep in touch.

He'd added maybe they could do a movie this afternoon.

Sara frowned. She didn't want to leave the resort. She liked being isolated from everyday life. Time enough to resume normal activities when her vacation was over. And it was passing too quickly—only a week left.

Eating some toast, she decided she could use a day to herself. To try to come to terms with her feeling with Alec, and make some definite plans for her own future.

By the time Alec returned, it was late morning. The rain had passed on. The sun was shining on the trees, sparkling on the droplets of water, and raising steam from the trees and porch roof.

"It turned out to be a nice day," Alec said as he entered the living room.

Sara looked up from her book and nodded.

He stopped. "Something wrong?"

She smiled brightly. "Not at all."

Hesitating a moment, he placed his briefcase and laptop down and moved to sit on one of the chairs.

"Want to go to the movie?"

"No, thanks, not today."

"Something *is* wrong."

She shook her head.

He narrowed his eyes. "Are you mad because I went off this morning?"

She shook her head again.

"Then what?"

Hoping the smile she was holding didn't look as insipid as it felt, she shrugged her shoulders. "Nothing's wrong. I'm tired today. My legs are a bit stiff from all that pedaling yesterday. I thought I'd just stay home and rest."

He was quiet for a while, studying her. Then he looked out the window. "If you don't want to go anywhere, you don't. I'm not going by myself."

"It is a pretty day, why don't you take a walk or maybe see if Mr. Simpson would like to go fishing this afternoon," she suggested.

"I might. Or I could explore those caves. You sure you don't want to go?"

"Not today. I'm going to eat lunch soon and then rest." After little sleep last night, and all the exercise she'd had yesterday, Sara was tired. But more than anything, she wanted some distance from Alec—before she did something stupid, like give away her feelings. The last thing she wanted was for him to suspect the turmoil plaguing her.

# CHAPTER NINE

DESPITE her suggestion, when Alec took off after lunch, Sara felt deserted. She watched him striding into the woods without a backward glance, and instantly missed him. He could have asked her again to go with him.

Not that she would have gone. The path still looked slick after the rain, and she was in no mood to be challenged today. She truly wanted to get some rest!

Going to her room to lie down, she drifted to sleep, but woke when the baby held a dance-a-thon. She read until the baby settled down, her eyes closing despite her interest in the book.

It was dark when Sara woke again and rain hammered on the roof. She looked through the doorway. She'd left the bedroom door ajar; the rest of the cabin was in darkness. Had Alec returned and then gone to the lodge for dinner because she was asleep?

Unlikely. He would have told her if he wasn't going to be home for dinner. And wouldn't he have left a light on?

Unless he'd gone before it got dark. He might have left another note.

She got up, used the bathroom and went downstairs. Switching on the light, she shivered. It was already cool in the cottage. The rain smeared the glass in the window, blown against it by the wind.

She looked for a note. Found none.

A tinge of worry pricked her. Where was Alec?

Searching the cottage took less than two minutes. No sign of him.

She looked outside. He couldn't still be on his walk. It was after eight and already completely dark! He'd probably gone to the lodge, and lost track of time.

Going to the phone, Sara lifted the receiver to call the lodge. She'd have him paged. Silence met her. The phone was dead. He could have tried calling her but she'd never have known.

She went to the kitchen to prepare something to eat. The rain beat against the window, adding to the gloom of the night.

By ten, Sara was truly getting worried.

She went to the door and opened it. Cold damp air swirled around. So much for summer weather! A person could get sick staying out in this kind of weather—especially with no shelter, or warm clothes.

The memory of Alec striding away that afternoon surfaced. He'd been wearing a cotton shirt, jeans and running shoes. And carrying a backpack with some snacks and water. No jacket, no hat, no rain gear. Had he gotten caught in the storm? Or worse, become dizzy and fallen, injuring himself further?

Sara slammed the door and looked around. What should she do? Grabbing a jacket, she dashed over to the Simpsons's cottage. Maybe their phone was working. Or maybe they'd seen him come home and then head for the lodge.

The place was dark. Knocking on the door, Sara waited impatiently, hoping for an answer. No response. She tried the handle. The door swung open and she stepped inside. The cottage had the same layout as hers, so she quickly located the phone to the front desk. The line was dead.

She almost ran back to her cottage. Closing the door to lean against it, she spotted his laptop, on the floor beside the sofa. He wouldn't have gone to the lodge without it.

She had two choices: try to find Alec, or walk to the main lodge and summon help. But trackers wouldn't know where to look for him. Could she walk to the lodge and then have energy enough to help in the search?

When the baby kicked, she patted her hand gently against her tummy. "The cavalry to the rescue. It's up to us, babykins. We've got to find your daddy."

In less than ten minutes, Sara had stuffed a backpack full of blankets and a change of clothes for Alec, a jacket and a first-aid kit. She prepared hot coffee and put it in a thermos. Grabbing a handful of snacks, she was ready. Donning her warmest clothes and a heavy jacket, she covered herself with a large plastic bag, and crammed on an old hat. She was as sheltered as she could get. Rain gear had not been high on her priority list when she packed for her vacation.

There were several flashlights around the cabin.

She gathered them all. Leaving a note in case Alec returned before she did, she set off.

Not five minutes into the trek Sara realized the trail was much more difficult to follow in the dark and the rain than on a sunny afternoon.

The floppy hat kept the worst of the rain from her face, but the wind dashed water every which way. The flashlight didn't offer much illumination. The soggy needles and spongy mud seemed to soak up what little light it gave. But she pushed on.

"Alec!" Sara called his name frequently. Stumbling once, she slowed down to cautiously find her way. She dare not allow herself to fall but urgency drove her on. She grew scared. The rain seemed unrelenting. The swaying trees appeared foreign and threatening. Yet Alec was somewhere out in the night, and she knew he'd come searching for her. How could she do less?

"Alec!"

How far was the meadow where they had shared a picnic? Had he gone all the way to the caves? Surely he would have started for the cabin when the rain threatened again.

Or had he thought the storm would pass quickly and was waiting it out safely in a dry cave?

"Alec!" Sara sloshed on. Her hand holding the flashlight trembled with cold. Blown rain seeped down the neck of her jacket despite her attempts to keep it at bay. Twice she slipped and ended up on her knees. But she kept at it. Her fear for Alec rose with each step.

"Alec!"

"Sara?" His voice was faint. From which direction?

She almost burst into tears. "Where are you?" She struggled on a little farther. She could see nothing besides the small circle of light in front of her feet.

"Alec, where are you?" She raised the flashlight and turned in a complete circle, hoping he could see the light.

"I see you. Be careful, it's slippery. Head a bit to your left."

She climbed the pathway, sliding, moving to the edge of the clearing where rocks and gravel gleamed in the faint light, rain running between them in rivulets.

"You're getting closer," his voice called.

In another five minutes she stopped. Rocks and boulders were strewn around like a careless toss from a giant hand.

"Alec?"

"I'm to your right, Sara. But be careful. It's slick."

Sweeping the flashlight around, she saw him.

"What happened?" she asked as she began to scramble over the rocks, using both hands from time to time to steady herself.

"I had a blasted dizziness attack, lost my footing and fell spraining my blasted ankle." He looked beyond her. "Are you alone?"

The pent-up worry exploded into relief. She felt almost giddy hearing his voice.

"Of course I'm alone, who did you think I'd pick up?"

"What the hell are you doing out in this weather in your condition? You could have been hurt!"

Picking her way gingerly through the rocks, she hastened toward him. The flashlight caught him in its beam.

"I was worried!"

"Sometimes, Sara, you need a keeper. Why didn't you get help from the lodge?"

"I tried to call, but the phone is out. If I couldn't call a Jeep, I'd have to walk and I didn't know if I could walk all that way, when I might meet you closer to the cabin."

"Dammit, I can't believe you came out in this."

She knelt beside him and threw herself into his arms. "What was I supposed to do? The Simpsons are gone and the other cabin is still vacant! All I could think about was you out here in this weather—without a jacket."

He held her tightly. "Damn fool thing to do."

"Are you sure a sprained ankle is all? Did you hit your head again or anything? Are you freezing?"

"I'll manage. You could have fallen and been hurt! You risked the baby's well-being, too."

"I'm a little cold, but fine otherwise. Truly. I was careful. I couldn't leave my baby's father out here, you'll get sick. Come on, we've got to get back to the cottage. If you lean on me, can you walk?"

"Not far." He rose and balanced on his left foot. Slowly he leaned on Sara. She braced herself for his weight. With the rocks to cross, then the muddy path and the pouring rain, there was no chance they'd make it back without further mishap.

"What's in here?" Alec asked nudging her backpack. He wasn't through with chastising her for her irresponsible behavior, but would wait before arguing the point with her. The deed was done, and truth to tell, he'd been struck by her fierce determination to aid her baby's father. She'd always been loyal.

"A blanket and some hot coffee, snacks."

"I've been fantasizing about a hot meal for hours. We aren't going to make it back tonight, Sara. The caves are nearby. We can find shelter from the rain and the wind at least. And if we have an ounce of luck we'll find a dry stick or two for a fire."

Winding through the rocks proved difficult. Alec knew how to get to the caves he'd spent that afternoon prowling. Slowly they made their way to the nearest one.

Once beneath the overhang, he released his grip on Sara's shoulder and sank down to the earthen floor with a muffled groan.

"Are you okay?" she asked, kneeling beside him, her hand touching his arm. If he wasn't, she hadn't a clue what to do about it.

"I will be soon. How about some of that coffee? I'm freezing!"

"I have more than that," she replied smugly, unzipping the backpack. Blankets spilled out, the thermos and socks. She handed him the thermos first then gathered his clothes.

"I brought you a change of clothes."

"You are a wise woman, Sara Blackstone."

"Hypothermia is dangerous—even in the summertime. And it's downright cold today."

He shrugged out of his shirt, tossed it to the side and pulled on the dry one.

Even as he was buttoning it up, she struggled with the laces of his shoes.

"Don't bother, I'll just toe them off."

"The injured foot, too?" she asked, working diligently.

"If we had scissors, you could cut the laces."

"You'll walk out of here tomorrow more easily if you have shoes that stay on your feet," she murmured. "There. One done. I wish the light was brighter."

He held the flashlight while she unfastened his other shoe and gently slipped it off. Lightly touching the cold, damp sock, she frowned. "Your ankle's swollen."

"But not much. Probably the cold wet sock helped to keep the swelling down."

"Get into the rest of the dry clothes while I look for wood," she said briskly, flicking on a second flashlight and scanning the interior of the cave. Rising, she shed the plastic bag, then wandered around, picking up a stick here and there, a twig, a handful of pine needles. She heard the rustling of his clothes and longed to offer help. But somehow she knew Alec would insist he could manage by himself.

"I'm decent now. Did you find any wood?" his amused voice called. She looked up, he was quite a distance away. The cave was much larger than she realized. Carrying her bounty, she hurried back to the dim circle of light where he sat.

His wet clothes were piled to the side. He was already huddled beneath one of the blankets.

Dumping the wood, she piled it up, then sat back on her heels. "There are matches in the backpack. In the first-aid kit."

"A Girl Scout, prepared for everything." Alec looked up and met her gaze. "Thanks, Sara, I owe you. But I still can't believe you risked your own safety and the baby's."

"You'd have come for me," she said simply.

"Yeah, but I'm not eight months pregnant."

"I was careful." She caught the matches he tossed to her and quickly lit some of the pine needles. They flared instantly and in only seconds a cheery fire was blazing before them. The light and the warmth were most welcome. For the first time since she realized Alec was missing, Sara began to relax.

"Come sit here." Alec patted the dry dirt beside him.

She crossed over and sat, hip to hip. He opened the blanket and draped it over her shoulders, then unscrewed the thermos of coffee.

Suddenly exhausted, Sara leaned against him.

"I was so scared," she said softly.

"I would have made it come morning. You knew I could have managed."

She nodded, not believing it for a minute. People died from hypothermia. Looking out into the black night she shivered. The rain continued to fall. Even with the fire the air was cool. Alec in just a wet shirt and jeans overnight would have had a tough time.

"Will you be able to walk back in the morning?" she asked after he'd finished the hot coffee.

"Depends. I'll see how the ankle is. If not, at least I'm warm and dry. You might have to hike back and get help."

The baby moved. When Sara instinctively placed her hand over her baby, Alec's hand covered hers, felt the movement of their child. For a split second Sara knew perfection.

"You never said what you wanted, Alec," she said softly, "a girl or a boy?"

"A healthy baby will suit me perfectly. I'm more concerned about its parents—I think kids need both parents. I had my father, but no mother."

"And I had no father after I was nine. At least in a divorce, mothers and fathers stay in contact with their children. You had the bad luck to have a mother who didn't for some reason. But that doesn't mean we can't work something out—if you want to be a part of the baby's life."

"Of course I do. I—" He fell silent.

"What?"

"Nothing." He withdrew his hand, and stared at the fire. "It's safer all the way around to never take a chance. That way, there's no heartache."

"That might be safer, but don't you think people would miss a lot?"

He shook his head, looking at her. "Are you happy with the way things turned out? If you had it to do over, would you still marry me?"

"I wish desperately that things had been different for us, but no, I don't think I would have chosen to skip it. What if we had been one of the lucky ones? What if we could have celebrated fifty years together like the Simpsons? That's what I was hoping for.'' The familiar ache settled in her heart. She'd had such high expectations when they married. How had they lost their way?

She yawned.

''I'm tired, too. Can you sleep?''

Sara nodded. ''Let me make another sweep of the cave for more wood. What we have now won't last all night. And I expect it'll be even colder come morning.''

In ten minutes she had scoured the cave for every bit of flammable material. Some they fed to the flame, the rest they stacked to the side to feed the fire during the night.

Urging her to lie down by the fire, Alec lay down beside her on one of the blankets, with the second covering them for warmth. Sara soon dozed off.

She awoke in the night to find herself wrapped in Alec's embrace. He'd opened his jacket, and drawn her right in against his heart. She felt toasty warm and comfortable. If only the dirt floor was a bit more forgiving!

Snuggling closer, she drifted back to sleep.

The cold woke her. Opening her eyes, she moved her legs slightly. Alec held her, only now her back was spooned against him, his chest a solid wall of warmth, his arms holding her loosely. Her legs were against his, but her feet were cold despite her shoes.

Slowly surveying the cave, she realized she could

see the ceiling, the far wall. Looking at the opening she saw it was well past dawn.

Sitting up, she shivered. The air felt cool, but the rain had stopped. The sky, what small portion she could see, was a deep blue. Sunshine shone through the tops of the trees.

"Good morning," Alec said.

She turned and smiled, her heart catching. He looked fantastic. His morning beard looked rugged and sexy. His tousled hair only had her yearning to brush it back. She probably looked like something the cat dragged in. His eyes caught hers and didn't let go.

"Wish we had some of that hot coffee left," she said, looking away feeling flustered.

"Time to head for home. I like camping out, but this is ridiculous."

Scrambling to her feet, Sara reached down and began to fold the blankets. The fire had gone out during the wee morning hours. There was nothing remaining but a small pile of ash.

Stuffing the backpack, she looked at his wet clothes.

"I'll take those in my backpack. No sense getting the blankets wet," he said, as if reading her mind.

Alec put on his shoes, wincing slightly as his injured foot slipped in.

"Are they dry?" she asked.

"No. But I set them close to the fire last night. They won't squirt water with every step, in any event."

Two minutes later they were ready to leave. Sara

gazed around the cave for a moment, then shook her head.

"This wasn't quite how I wanted to go exploring. I expected pirates had it warmer."

"But I wouldn't want to play pirate with anyone else but you," Alec said gruffly as he tried putting weight on his injured ankle.

"Wait!" She came over and offered her shoulder.

"It's better today," he said.

"But it won't be by the time we reach home. Favor it as much as you can. It's a long hike. I can still go ahead and bring back help."

"I'll manage. Let's go."

The Simpsons saw them limping in and hurried to offer assistance. Within minutes, Alec was in their cabin, the front desk had been called and a Jeep requested to take him to the first-aid station. Mrs. Simpson plied them with sweet hot tea and delicious cinnamon rolls she had baked fresh that morning.

"I'm so sorry we weren't home last night. We went to the lodge for dinner and stayed for dancing," she explained after Sara had told of her efforts to get help.

"We did that the other night," Sara murmured. "There was no way you could have known we'd need help, or that the phones would be out."

Rosemarie Simpson was obviously going to fret about the entire situation. "I can't believe you went out in that weather!"

"Which is exactly what I told her," Alec said grimly.

"I'm tough," Sara said with a grin.

Alec narrowed his eyes, but said nothing.

It was lunchtime before they finished at the resort's first-aid station. Alec's ankle had been wrapped, more pain pills doled out. Sara had also been checked and pronounced in fine health.

The lodge management had urged them to have lunch—on the house—before returning to their cottage.

"Trying to make sure we don't file a complaint," Alec commented cynically as they sat near the tall windows overlooking the lake.

"Well, I think it's a nice gesture on their part. They can't be held responsible for the weather, or your dizzy spell," Sara said. She glanced around and then looked at Alec. "And brave on their part. We don't look quite as tidy as most of the diners."

He met her eyes. "I think you look beautiful."

Sara's eyes widened. Her breath caught in her throat. She couldn't believe how often he told her, and how she cherished every compliment.

When lunch was finished, they walked to the front of the lodge to get a Jeep, Alec leaning heavily on the cane provided.

"Don't you want to dash into the guest office for a few minutes and catch up on work?" Sara asked as they waited for one of the colorful vehicles to take them to the cabin.

Alec shook his head. "Not today."

Surprised, Sara wondered why the change. Any other time and he'd have insisted. Now he was turning his back on an opportunity to work. Amazing!

"What do you plan to do at the cottage?" she asked.

"Lie out on the hammock and not move until time for supper" was the quick response. He looked at her searchingly. "Want to join me?"

Before she could respond, the Jeep pulled to a squealing stop and the young driver hopped out. "Take you to your cabin?"

By the time she'd finished showering, Sara was exhausted. The thought of climbing into the hammock with Alec was tantalizing, especially since their time together was growing short. But she knew she needed rest and would do better in her own bed.

She was asleep before he finished his own shower.

Alec checked on Sara, disappointed to find her fast asleep on her bed. He'd wanted her to lie with him on the hammock. Twice now they'd slept together, and each time he woke, he wondered why he expected to find her beside him all the next times he awoke.

It was vacation madness, nothing more. They'd spent some time together, had some fun. For a few days he remembered the two of them as they'd been when courting. But he knew once back at work, he'd be engulfed in the day-to-day urgency and not have the time to devote to her that she demanded. She'd been wise to leave him when she did.

But the nagging feeling of something being wrong didn't abate.

He lay on the hammock and stared up through the tall trees to the deep blue sky. He was lying to himself. He would always think about her—to wonder how she was doing, especially with the baby. To wonder if she was all right living as a single parent. Visits wouldn't be enough.

Moving, he accidentally knocked his right foot and pain shot up his leg. Some vacation, he thought wryly. He was more banged up than when he arrived. Stacking his hands beneath his head, he ignored the cast as he thought over the past couple of weeks. Meeting Sara had been a surprise, but it had turned out all right. They were getting along.

Of course nothing had been settled. Would pushing her to make a decision concerning their situation change the dynamics? Was she deliberately holding off until the end of their stay?

He'd done a lot of thinking when sitting in the rain. Some of the conclusions he'd arrived at, he didn't like.

Alec stared into space for a long time before finally falling asleep.

When he awoke, Rosemary Simpson was sitting nearby. "I didn't want to waken you, but wanted to invite you and Sara to dinner tonight. Neither of you will feel like cooking after your adventures. And it's not that far to our cabin. If you like, Paul can come to help you over. Or we can bring dinner to your place."

He sat on the edge of the hammock and tested his ankle.

"I think I can manage to get as far as your cabin. It feels better already." He looked up. "Thanks."

"I still feel distressed we weren't home last night when Sara needed us! Neighbors should rally around in troubled times."

"It turned out all right," Alec said.

"Yes, but she could have been injured, or hurt the baby. I can't believe she went out like that. She must love you so much. I know she must have been frantic with worry! I would have been if something happened to Paul. You two come about seven."

He watched her walk away.

*She must love you so much!* He'd had that once, and carelessly taken it for granted. Ignored his wife until her feelings had died and everything changed. He no longer had the love she'd so generously bestowed before they married.

Mrs. Simpson had been wrong. Sara had come looking for him simply because she knew where to find him. She would have done the same for anyone in trouble.

I couldn't leave my baby's father out here, she'd said. He wished she'd just said she couldn't leave her baby's father.

Rising, he headed for the cottage. He wanted to see her again, to make sure she was not suffering any aftereffects from exposure. The first-aid nurse had pronounced her fit, but he needed to make sure.

The mouthwatering fragrance of chocolate chip cookies filled the air as he drew near the back door. He stood in the opening for a long moment, watching Sara bustle around the kitchen. Here was proof, if he needed it, that she'd suffered no ill effects. Two racks of cookies were cooling. She opened the oven door and swiftly withdrew a cookie sheet. Turning, she caught sight of him and smiled.

Did he imagine a sparkle in her eyes? A hint of happiness at the sight of him?

Probably.

"Hi, want some fresh-baked cookies?" she asked, setting the hot baking sheet down on the counter.

He shook his head. "What I want is you."

Crossing the room in three steps, he drew her into his arms and kissed her. Her lips were soft and warm. Her skin smelled of flowers and chocolate. Her body seemed to come alive in his arms, or maybe it was his own coming alive. She filled his senses. He couldn't get enough of her.

And he still had to tell her he was leaving in two days.

# CHAPTER TEN

SARA had mixed emotions when Alec told her about accepting the Simpsons's invitation to dinner. She was glad not to have to prepare dinner but she resented the fact she'd have to share Alec. She would have preferred to keep him all to herself.

Such a selfish wish, she thought as she brushed her short hair and put on a trace of makeup. Wearing a sundress, and taking a sweater for when the evening grew cool, she descended the stairs. Alec stood at the doorway, gazing out toward the lake. He leaned slightly on the cane.

Surprised, Sara realized she expected him to be on the sofa reading one of the briefs or jotting notes. Had he spent the entire day doing nothing about work? Or had he handled those tasks while she napped?

He heard her and spun around, watching her descend the final steps. She felt self-conscious and very aware of how sexy Alec looked. He'd picked up a tan since he'd arrived and the tight look around his eyes was gone. His hair was a bit longer than he usually wore it, but it only added to his rugged good looks.

Except for the cast, and the cane, he looked fit and strong and ready to slay dragons.

Only, the dragons in their lives, she thought sadly, were the ones they'd devised.

"Let's not stay late," Alec said.

Surprised, she nodded, her mood lightening. Did he want to spend time with her like she wanted to be with him?

"That's fine. Though we can't just eat and run."

He raised an eyebrow. "Sure we can. I'll develop a dizzy spell."

"That won't work," she said almost laughing at his teasing tone. "You'd just have to lie down there until it passed and that could be hours."

"Then you get very sleepy and demand to go home to bed."

She looked away wishing fervently that going home to bed meant sharing one with Alec again. She missed his presence in the night. Missed the closeness they'd had in the first few months of their marriage.

As they walked the short distance to the Simpsons's cottage, Sara began to wonder if she should have put more effort into sharing his vacation. Taking the cell phone had worked. Alec had yet to ask for it back.

And he had not stopped at the guest office either yesterday or today.

Struck by his odd behavior, Sara didn't have any time to explore the ramifications. The elderly couple greeted them and in only moments they were sitting beneath the trees, the delicious aroma of barbecue pork filling the air.

During the evening Sara noticed Alec's gaze on

her frequently. She raised her eyebrows once in silent question, but he just shook his head and looked away.

It was after ten when they returned to their own cottage. Sara had enjoyed herself and suspected Alec had as well. For her it seemed to prove he was capable of avoiding reference of work. What would he be like if he kept more regular hours and developed other interests? Such as a renewed interest in her and in their baby.

"They're nice, aren't they?" she asked as he switched on the lamps.

"Yes. They seem to have a lot in common, wouldn't you say?"

"I guess. I loved hearing them talk about their family traditions. I want that. The expectation, the anticipation, the contentment in doing some things on a regular basis. I expect to establish a lot with the baby."

"Do you think we have anything in common, Sara?" he asked.

She hesitated, leaning against the banister. "We didn't make enough effort, did we, Alec?" she asked wistfully. "We both had our careers already started when we married, and both tried to keep on the same way we'd been before. By the time I realized I wanted something different, it was too late."

She sat down on the third step, and rested her elbows on her legs, her chin in her hand. "I think we should have met the Simpsons long ago, or someone like them. Someone to give us some suggestions."

She was pensive for a moment. "As to something in common, we liked fishing together."

He shrugged, his gaze steady.

She wrinkled her nose again, feeling close to tears. Did they truly have nothing in common, nothing on which to build a life together? She loved him! She wanted to spend her life with him. Was it too impossible?

"We could go again tomorrow. And if your ankle is better in the next day or two, we could go to the lodge for lunch and go wading at the beach. It's shallow enough that the water might warm a degree or two above the rest of the lake."

He shook his head. "I'm leaving, Sara."

Her heart skipped a beat. "Leaving? When?"

"Day after tomorrow. I have an appointment the next day to see my doctor."

She stared at him, feeling shell-shocked. "But you'll be back, right? Wyatt reserved this place for three weeks. We'd still have the weekend."

At his silence, she jumped up. "No, of course you won't be back. Why make the trip out here a second time? This way you'll be right in Boston, can stop into the office and get all caught up with your unexpected witness, with the new strategy and plunge right back into your old routine." She turned and ran up the stairs, slamming the bedroom door behind her.

The thought of tears fled as anger consumed her. How could she have been foolish enough to think they had a chance together, to think Alec had changed just because he managed a day away from work? She paced the small confines of the room, anger building.

Anger, or a tremendous sadness at the loss of a future that had, for a few days, dangled so enticingly in front of her?

She stopped and took a deep breath. Tomorrow was all she had. One last day. Then the emptiness of a lonely future.

The baby stirred and she patted it gently.

"If tomorrow is all we have it's going to be the best day ever!" she vowed.

Early the next morning, Sara slipped across the hall and banged on Alec's door.

"Hmm? What?" The door flung open, Alec looked ready to dash out into the world. "What? Sara, are you all right?"

She smiled up at him, struck anew by the sexiness that seemed to call directly to her.

"Yes. Time to go fishing. The best time to catch them is dawn, right?"

He rubbed his hand through his hair. Despite her best efforts, she couldn't keep her gaze from slipping from that tousled dark hair down across broad shoulders to where his waist narrowed. The pajama pants he wore rode low on his hips. She was tempted to reach out and touch the expanse that beckoned. Clenching her hands tightly to resist temptation, she forced her eyes to meet his.

Then, unable to stop herself, she let her fingertips brush against his chest. Just once more couldn't hurt.

He captured her hand and drew her into his arms.

That warm chest was pressed against her and he lowered his mouth to cover hers, kiss hers. He was warm and hard and sexy and she wanted him more than anything else in life.

His morning beard felt familiar and dear against her cheeks. His lips were persuasive and compelling and she returned his kiss with all the fervor in her. She loved this man.

Slowly he ended the kiss and looked into her eyes.

"I don't want breakfast, or to go fishing," he said in that low, husky, seductive voice that melted across her nerve endings like hot syrup.

If she only dared offer an alternative to breakfast—like returning to bed together and spending the day there.

And why not? They were still married. Had enjoyed each other's company for more than two weeks. Had touched, kissed, laughed, danced and shared adventures. Why not one last adventure—one to last a lifetime?

Her eyes gazed into his, her heart caught in her throat. Could she suggest such a thing? Once voiced, there'd be no going back.

He watched her warily, as slowly his expression changed. Desire flared in his eyes. Maybe she didn't have to say anything at all. Maybe he already knew.

"Sara?" he said softly.

"If you don't want to go fishing, what do you want to do?"

"This." He kissed her, drawing her against him as if she was the only thing in his world, and he had to hold on lest it be wrest away.

Maybe Sara could show him how much he was going to miss over the years when he chose work over play!

Her heart slammed into high gear as he deepened the kiss. His hands moved across her back, cupping her bottom, lifting her to rub against his chest. She could feel the strength of his muscles, of his desire.

"Come with me, Sara, and let's explore what we have in common," he said against her mouth, spinning slowly as he eased them across the bedroom to the rumpled bed.

She tried to imprint every move, every touch, every brush of his fingertips, so down through the years she would be able to relive today's perfection.

Slowly they sank onto the mattress, locked in each other's arms.

"I want you, Sara," he mumbled against her throat as his kisses caused shivering delight.

*I love you,* she replied in silent response, trying to show him with everything she had.

The heat of the sunlight streaming in through the high window mingled with the heat from Alec's body. His mouth did wicked things to hers, making her think of midnight, and tangled sheets and the wild love they used to make when first married.

Tears came when she thought of the past and how they'd lost their way. But she refused to let them fall. She reveled in his touch, in the sensations that built and filled her.

Her hands skimmed over his skin, relishing her right to tantalize, caress, stroke. She was on fire, and only this man could quench her need.

Instead of quenching it, however, he fed the flames. Every kiss set her senses spinning out of control. Every feathery brush of his fingers across her skin sent waves of exquisite delight shimmering through her. When the tension built to dangerous levels, he still urged her higher and higher, until she exploded with heat and pleasure and love.

His own shout a second later assured her that pregnancy not withstanding, she and Alec did indeed have something in common.

Slowly she drifted back to earth. Savoring each ripple and impression. Wishing time would stand still.

Alec moved to her side, drawing her close to his chest, brushing back her damp hair and kissing her forehead.

She watched him dreamily, wondering if he was going to fall sleep, memorizing the way his hair fell, the way his chest rose and fell as his breathing deepened.

His eyes opened.

"What will you do when I'm gone?" he asked, brushing back her hair again, letting his fingers linger.

A definite reminder they had only hours left together. Pushing away the hurt, she shrugged. "I'll carry on like I planned to when I first arrived. I expected to be alone on this vacation, you know. I'll be fine. It's only for a few days more."

"Don't go to the caves alone."

"I'll be fine, Alec. Don't worry about me."

He closed his eyes and clamped down on the urge

to argue with her. She was right, he shouldn't worry about her. But he would. Hadn't these two weeks proved that she was not beyond taking risks? She walked around the lake by herself. He hadn't thought about how potentially dangerous it could be until he'd run into difficulties on his own solo hike.

She could fall and no one would have a clue where she was. Or even know to look for her.

He'd speak to the Simpsons, make sure they kept an eye on her until she left.

Would being on her own again give her time to think about legally ending their marriage? He frowned. He didn't want to think about that. Though what he thought she'd do was beyond him at the moment.

Truth to tell, he'd been a bit surprised she hadn't already filed for divorce. Maybe she'd go ahead with her plans once he left. Nothing had changed, had it? He was who he was and she wanted more than he could give. Right?

Not liking the trend of his thoughts, he sat up and forced them away.

She looked at him. "Loving time over?"

"No, I'll be back. Don't move."

She smiled at the comment, and Alec wanted to grab it and hold on to it forever. He wanted to hear her laughter again, see the light sparkling in her eyes. The single thing he missed most in his empty apartment was the echo of her laughter. Or maybe it was her scent.

Or was it the nights in bed, talking far into the dark that he missed most?

Damn, he'd had months to get over her. And done fine. Work was demanding enough to take all his energy. Once he returned he'd make sure he was kept busy—to drive away the ghosts of Sara again.

He rose and went downstairs to get them some breakfast. He didn't know where the idea of breakfast in bed had come from, but he had to act quickly before giving into needs. He wanted his pretty wife with a desire that seemed to grow hourly. Never mind they'd made passionate love not a half hour before. He still wanted her.

Maybe he could keep her in his bed all day!

Anything to delay beginning the separation process all over again.

She was surprised, and delighted, by breakfast in bed. They talked and laughed, and later snuggled together to discuss names for the baby.

When he kissed her again, she turned willingly, eagerly into his arms.

The hours flew by until wispy clouds reflected the rosy shades of sunset, gradually fading into darkness. They watched from his window, still entwined in each other's arms.

"I'm glad we had this time together," Sara said.

"Me, too." One part of him didn't want it to end. Another knew he had to escape if he was to ever have a chance to regain his equilibrium. Being around Sara brought dreams that he knew were futile.

"What time do you leave in the morning?" she asked at last.

"The Jeep will be here at eight to pick me up. I

catch the eight-thirty shuttle from the lodge to the airport.''

''Mmmm.''

For a moment he feared tears and recriminations. But Sara had never tried any female tricks to get her way. She'd always been blunt and open and forthright.

And Alec suddenly felt like a failure. He'd not measured up.

He gathered her closer. ''Stay the night with me.''

She nodded. ''I'll get up and fix you breakfast.''

''No, sleep in. I'll get something at the airport.''

He knew it was time to make the break. Time to move back to the life he knew and had chosen. This vacation had merely been a segment of dream time. Real life didn't function like this. It was time he let go and returned.

Despite what he'd said, Sara rose when he did and had coffee ready by the time Alec came down from packing the next morning.

She smiled, determined to make it through these next few minutes. It was almost eight. He'd be gone soon.

''It's not breakfast, just coffee. But I know you like it first thing and it'll tide you over until you get to the airport.''

''Thanks.'' He took the mug and sipped, his eyes drinking her in.

She hoped the shorts and pink shirt flattered her. Pink was her best color, she often thought. She'd put on makeup and looked her best. Let him remember her looking this way.

"Oh, here." She handed him the cell phone. "You might need this."

"I'll call you when you get back to Boston," he said, tucking it into his pocket.

She nodded, the smile feeling forced and as artificial as plastic. But she refused to let it waiver.

"We never decided on names," she said, then swallowed hard. They had spent hours discussing various names, then became sidetracked with kisses.

She would not think about that, either. In fact, she dare not think about any thing until he'd left. She could get through this!

A horn tooted. The Jeep had arrived.

Sara took a deep breath and widened her smile. "Have a good trip, Alec. I hope the doctor says everything is fine. I'll just stay in here."

"I'll call you." He set the cup on the counter and took the two steps that separated them, brushing his lips across hers. He stared into her eyes for a long moment.

"You're going to be all right?"

"Fine. Go on now, you don't want to miss your plane."

He nodded once, then left.

She listened to the sound of his footsteps across the wooden floor as he headed for the front door. A few moments later the door closed. Silence.

Tears began to trail down her cheeks and she caught back a sob. Smiling was no longer an option. Her heart felt as if it were shattering into a million pieces. She turned and went out to sit on the back stoop. Leaning against the railing, she let the tears come, hot and fast. Rubbing her chest, she longed for the ache to subside. He was gone. Their idyllic vacation was over.

And nothing had changed. She was alone. He'd chosen work over her yet again. Which was foolish; he hadn't had to make that choice again—he had set it in stone long ago.

She blew her nose and gazed at the lonely hammock. She felt achy and out of sorts. Her back hurt. Too much lovemaking yesterday and last night, she thought wryly. Or could anyone ever have too much?

Determined not to let his departure ruin the rest of her vacation, she packed a lunch, grabbed her backpack and headed for the meadow. She'd enjoy the rest of her vacation or know the reason why.

Halfway up the path, the nagging ache in her back grew stronger. Lengthening her stride, she thought walking might ease the muscles, stretch them out a bit. For a while she felt better.

Stopping for lunch at their meadow, she considered exploring the caves, until a sharp pain in her lower abdomen had her clutching for relief.

"Ow, that hurt," she murmured, settling back on the blanket. Giving up the idea of exploring the caves, she began to wonder if something more than feeling tired from making love was causing her problems.

Ten minutes later a sharp contraction hit. There was no confusing that.

"Oh, God," she said softly. She couldn't be going

into labor. She wasn't even due for three weeks, and everyone knew first babies came late!

But before she could pack up her picnic lunch, another contraction caused her to double over.

Great, she was an hour's hike from a phone, alone on the side of a mountain, going into labor and no one in the world had an idea where she was!

# CHAPTER ELEVEN

"SARA?"

She looked up. Now she was hallucinating. She could have sworn it was Alec's voice. But he was halfway to Boston.

Through the tears of frustration and fear, she saw him. He wasn't in Boston, he was striding toward her, across the meadow, the breeze tossing his hair every which way as he drew closer and closer.

"Alec?" She burst into tears. "Alec, I'm in labor!"

"What? Sara, what are you doing here?" He knelt beside her, placing his hand on her stomach, feeling the tightness, his other hand brushing back her hair, cupping her chin.

"Are you out of your mind? Didn't I specifically say you weren't to go off by yourself?"

"I wouldn't be by myself if you hadn't left," she snapped, then stifled a groan as another contraction gripped.

"I'm here now, and we have to get you to a hospital."

"Great idea. Any plans how to do that?"

"How far apart are the contractions?"

"I don't know, they seem to come right after each other. I didn't bring my watch. Why did you come back?"

Once the contraction eased, she could think clearly. "Did you forget something?"

He nodded gravely. "You."

He sat beside her on the blanket and pulled her onto his lap, covering her lips with his. The kiss was wonderful, fiery, exciting, and most thorough.

Sara was breathing hard when he rested his forehead on hers, then tensed as another contraction hit.

*"Ohhhh,"* she moaned softly. "This hurts!"

He glanced at his watch, frowning. "We have to get going, Sara. I can't believe you came out here when you were going into labor."

"I didn't do it deliberately!" She slowly gained her feet with Alec's help. Standing cautiously, she took a deep breath. Every respite was welcomed.

"Can you walk?"

She almost laughed. "If I can't, do you plan to carry me? Us?"

"If I have to."

"I can walk, at least for a while. They said in the birthing classes that walking during labor often helps."

"I suspect they didn't mean hiking in the Adirondacks."

"Hmmm." She braced for another contraction. *"Ohhhhhh!"*

He encircled her shoulders, giving her something to lean against and checked his watch. "Eight minutes apart. Does that mean anything to you?"

She shrugged, unable to do anything but fight against the pain. When it passed, she pushed against him to stand alone. Licking her lips, she said,

"They'll come closer and closer together, but the whole process takes hours. We'll have time to get back."

She hoped they did. She couldn't imagine delivering her baby in the woods!

Quickly gathering the remnants of her picnic, Alec stuffed everything into the backpack and took her arm, leading the way toward the cabin.

"Why are you here?" she asked as they walked slowly down the slight incline.

"I couldn't leave. I got all the way to the airport and realized it. So I came back. Then I couldn't find you in the cottage. Mrs. Simpson said you'd headed this way."

She stopped and almost doubled over. He held her as she waited out the contraction.

"Still eight minutes," he murmured once she was able to walk again. "Are you sure you can be walking? I don't want the baby to drop out on his head."

She giggled softly, squeezing his hand. "Thank you for coming back. What would I do without you?"

"Hold that thought, Sara."

"What do you mean?"

"Where should I start?"

"At the beginning?" she suggested, hoping whatever he had to say would take her mind off the growing fear she wouldn't make it to the hospital in time for her baby's birth.

"I wish I knew where that was. When I first saw you and you took away my breath? When I knew I wanted you in my life forever? Or was the beginning of this part when after we were married I fell back into old habits. I'd been alone a long time, Sara. I think I never cultivated the ability to share. I thought I had to give you everything, so I worked harder to earn more.''

"All I wanted was you.''

"These past few months have been hell. The apartment is twice as empty than before. Your ghost is everywhere.''

She gave a watery giggle. "Alec, I'm not dead. How can I have a ghost?''

"I don't know, but you haunted the place. I stayed away more than ever to avoid going into our empty home. Worked longer hours to drive you from my mind.''

"Wouldn't it have been easier to just invite me back?'' she asked.

"And change my lifestyle when I was so sure you were the one wrong to expect me to alter the way I lived?''

"Well, when you put it that way...''

"Instead *I* was wrong. We both needed to alter our single lives to accommodate our married one. But me more than you.''

*"Ohhhhh!''* She bent over again, braced against her husband. He held her securely, waiting patiently. He never gave a hint of worry and Sara drew strength from him.

"And when did you come up with this notion that we might both need to change?'' she asked, breathing hard, almost daring to hope. Nodding a moment later, they stepped out again.

"The other night when I sat in the pouring rain. I did a lot of thinking then. You knew how dangerous it was to be exposed to the elements like that. I think I would have made it, but what if I hadn't? What if I had died?''

She shivered at his words. She'd had more than a few frantic thoughts along those lines. What would the world be like if Alec wasn't in it?

"My life isn't worth much without you. I'm like an automaton, going through the motions. Work is no longer a passion, but a drug—to dull the ache of your leaving. And you were right, the Boston legal system won't come to a halt with my absence. I like to think I make a contribution, but so do all the others in the D.A.'s office. We're a team, not soloists.''

"I think they'd sorely miss you if you were gone. But not collapse,'' she said.

"We'll test it.''

"How?''

"First of all, I'll take the time off the doctor recommended. I'll learn to delegate more. I've found I like doing other things—if I do them with you.''

Her heart rate soared. Throwing caution to the wind, Sara stopped to wind her arms around his neck and hugged him close.

"I love you, Alec,'' she whispered.

"I love you, Sara—more than I ever thought possible.'' He kissed her, just like she'd been hoping he would.

*"Ohhhh,"* she broke off, panting with the pain.

He checked his watch. "Much as I like dalliance,

I think we better hurry, sweetheart. You've now dropped to six minutes.''

The remaining trip to the cabin passed in a haze for Sara. She clung to Alec, walking between contractions, growing more and more scared with each constriction that she was destined to have her baby right where she stood.

She was jubilant when she spotted the cabin through the trees. In only minutes they were inside and Alec on the phone with the lodge. By then the contractions were only moments apart.

"Upstairs and into bed, sweetheart," he said, coming to urge her up.

"I'm not going up any stairs," she panted, gripping his arm tightly. "I want to go to the hospital."

"They've called for an ambulance, but I don't think it'll arrive before the baby. You'll be more comfortable in bed. Can you make it?''

She looked at the stairs and shook her head.

Without a word, he swept her into his arms and carried her up to her room.

"Your ankle, arm, *ohhh.*"

"I'm fine. Let's get those shorts off."

Before the next contraction could strike, he had her clothes off, a light nightgown on and into bed.

Alec rested his palm on the swelling that was their baby. "Let's give our baby a two-parent home, Sara. Come back to me. I promise to put you before work from now on! We'll establish traditions, find common interests and build our marriage rock-solid."

"Are you doing this just for the baby?" she asked.

"No. I'm doing it for me and you, for us. I have

fallen in love with you all over again. I know what life is like without you. I want to see what we can build together. Even if there wasn't a baby, I'd want you back!''

Dare she trust her heart?

''Take a chance with me, sweetheart. I promise to put you first. You were right. We have enough material things. But spending time together—that's priceless. I love you, Sara. I want you back!''

She flung her arms around his neck and held on tightly. No one knew what the future held, but she was willing to risk everything for the man she loved. She laughed with the sheer joy of the moment. She loved Alec and he loved her! For the first time in months, the future looked bright with promise.

''Yes, yes, yes! *Ohhhh!* Alec, I think the baby's coming!''

''Then let him come, sweetheart, I think we're ready.''

The ambulance arrived thirty minutes later. By then Angela Blackstone had announced her arrival into the world with lusty cries. Her parents had tears in their eyes as they participated in the birth of their child. Fear and concerns were swept away as nature took control and an easy delivery went smoothly.

Wrapping his daughter in a soft, clean towel, Alec sat beside Sara on the bed while the Emergency Medical Technicians checked his wife. Pronouncing her in perfect condition, he let the wave of relief pour over him.

Leaning closer, he kissed her softly.

"I love you," he said. "Now and forever."

"Now and forever," she repeated, her heart aglow with happiness.

## *Marriages meant to last!*

They've already said "I do," but what happens
when their promise to love, honor and cherish
is put to the test?

Emotions run high as husbands and wives
discover how precious—and fragile—
their wedding vows are....
Will true love keep them together—forever?

Look out in Harlequin Romance® for:

**HUSBAND FOR A YEAR**
**Rebecca Winters** (August, #3665)

**THE MARRIAGE TEST**
**Barbara McMahon** (September, #3669)

**HIS TROPHY WIFE**
**Leigh Michaels** (October, #3672)

**THE WEDDING DEAL**
**Janelle Denison** (November, #3678)

**PART-TIME MARRIAGE**
**Jessica Steele** (December, #3680)

*Available wherever Harlequin books are sold.*

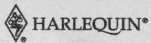

*Harlequin truly does
make any time special. . . .
This year we are celebrating
weddings in style!*

To help us celebrate, we want you to tell us how wearing the Harlequin wedding gown will make your wedding day special. As the grand prize, Harlequin will offer one lucky bride the chance to **"Walk Down the Aisle"** in the Harlequin wedding gown!

## There's more...

For her honeymoon, she and her groom will spend five nights at the **Hyatt Regency Maui.** As part of this five-night honeymoon at the hotel renowned for its romantic attractions, the couple will enjoy a candlelit dinner for two in Swan Court, a sunset sail on the hotel's catamaran, and duet spa treatments.

To enter, please write, in, 250 words or less, how wearing the Harlequin wedding gown will make your wedding day special. The entry will be judged based on its emotionally compelling nature, its originality and creativity, and its sincerity. This contest is open to Canadian and U.S. residents only and to those who are 18 years of age and older. There is no purchase necessary to enter. Void where prohibited. See further contest rules attached. Please send your entry to:

### Walk Down the Aisle Contest

| In Canada | In U.S.A. |
|---|---|
| P.O. Box 637 | P.O. Box 9076 |
| Fort Erie, Ontario | 3010 Walden Ave. |
| L2A 5X3 | Buffalo, NY 14269-9076 |

You can also enter by visiting www.eHarlequin.com
***Win the Harlequin wedding gown and the vacation of a lifetime!***
The deadline for entries is October 1, 2001.

PHWDACONT1

# HARLEQUIN WALK DOWN THE AISLE TO MAUI CONTEST 1197
## OFFICIAL RULES
### NO PURCHASE NECESSARY TO ENTER

1. To enter, follow directions published in the offer to which you are responding. Contest begins April 2, 2001, and ends on October 1, 2001. Method of entry may vary. Mailed entries must be postmarked by October 1, 2001, and received by October 8, 2001.

2. Contest entry may be, at times, presented via the Internet, but will be restricted solely to residents of certain geographic areas that are disclosed on the Web site. To enter via the Internet, if permissible, access the Harlequin Web site (www.eHarlequin.com) and follow the directions displayed online. Online entries must be received by 11:59 p.m. E.S.T. on October 1, 2001.

   In lieu of submitting an entry online, enter by mail by hand-printing (or typing) on an 8½" x 11" plain piece of paper, your name, address (including zip code), Contest number/name and in 250 words or fewer, why winning a Harlequin wedding dress would make your wedding day special. Mail via first-class mail to: Harlequin Walk Down the Aisle Contest 1197, (in the U.S.) P.O. Box 9076, 3010 Walden Avenue, Buffalo, NY 14269-9076, (in Canada) P.O. Box 637, Fort Erie, Ontario L2A 5X3, Canada.

   Limit one entry per person, household address and e-mail address. Online and/or mailed entries received from persons residing in geographic areas in which Internet entry is not permissible will be disqualified.

3. Contests will be judged by a panel of members of the Harlequin editorial, marketing and public relations staff based on the following criteria:

   * Originality and Creativity—50%
   * Emotionally Compelling—25%
   * Sincerity—25%

   In the event of a tie, duplicate prizes will be awarded. Decisions of the judges are final.

4. All entries become the property of Torstar Corp. and will not be returned. No responsibility is assumed for lost, late, illegible, incomplete, inaccurate, nondelivered or misdirected mail or misdirected e-mail, for technical, hardware or software failures of any kind, lost or unavailable network connections, or failed, incomplete, garbled or delayed computer transmission or any human error which may occur in the receipt or processing of the entries in this Contest.

5. Contest open only to residents of the U.S. (except Puerto Rico) and Canada, who are 18 years of age or older, and is void wherever prohibited by law; all applicable laws and regulations apply. Any litigation within the Province of Quebec respecting the conduct or organization of a publicity contest may be submitted to the Régie des alcools, des courses et des jeux for a ruling. Any litigation respecting the awarding of a prize may be submitted to the Régie des alcools, des courses et des jeux only for the purpose of helping the parties reach a settlement. Employees and immediate family members of Torstar Corp. and D. L. Blair, Inc., their affiliates, subsidiaries and all other agencies, entities and persons connected with the use, marketing or conduct of this Contest are not eligible to enter. Taxes on prizes are the sole responsibility of winners. Acceptance of any prize offered constitutes permission to use winner's name, photograph or other likeness for the purposes of advertising, trade and promotion on behalf of Torstar Corp., its affiliates and subsidiaries without further compensation to the winner, unless prohibited by law.

6. Winners will be determined no later than November 15, 2001, and will be notified by mail. Winners will be required to sign and return an Affidavit of Eligibility form within 15 days after winner notification. Noncompliance within that time period may result in disqualification and an alternative winner may be selected. Winners of trip must execute a Release of Liability prior to ticketing and must possess required travel documents (e.g. passport, photo ID) where applicable. Trip must be completed by November 2002. No substitution of prize permitted by winner. Torstar Corp. and D. L. Blair, Inc., their parents, affiliates, and subsidiaries are not responsible for errors in printing or electronic presentation of Contest, entries and/or game pieces. In the event of printing or other errors which may result in unintended prize values or duplication of prizes, all affected game pieces or entries shall be null and void. If for any reason the Internet portion of the Contest is not capable of running as planned, including infection by computer virus, bugs, tampering, unauthorized intervention, fraud, technical failures, or any other causes beyond the control of Torstar Corp. which corrupt or affect the administration, secrecy, fairness, integrity or proper conduct of the Contest, Torstar Corp. reserves the right, at its sole discretion, to disqualify any individual who tampers with the entry process and to cancel, terminate, modify or suspend the Contest or the Internet portion thereof. In the event of a dispute regarding an online entry, the entry will be deemed submitted by the authorized holder of the e-mail account submitted at the time of entry. Authorized account holder is defined as the natural person who is assigned to an e-mail address by an Internet access provider, online service provider or other organization that is responsible for arranging e-mail address for the domain associated with the submitted e-mail address. **Purchase or acceptance of a product offer does not improve your chances of winning.**

7. Prizes: (1) Grand Prize—A Harlequin wedding dress (approximate retail value: $3,500) and a 5-night/6-day honeymoon trip to Maui, HI, including round-trip air transportation provided by Maui Visitors Bureau from Los Angeles International Airport (winner is responsible for transportation to and from Los Angeles International Airport) and a Harlequin Romance Package, including hotel accomodations (double occupancy) at the Hyatt Regency Maui Resort and Spa, dinner for (2) two at Swan Court, a sunset sail on Kiele V and a spa treatment for the winner (approximate retail value: $4,000); (5) Five runner-up prizes of a $1000 gift certificate to selected retail outlets to be determined by Sponsor (retail value $1000 ea.). Prizes consist of only those items listed as part of the prize. Limit one prize per person. All prizes are valued in U.S. currency.

8. For a list of winners (available after December 17, 2001) send a self-addressed, stamped envelope to: Harlequin Walk Down the Aisle Contest 1197 Winners, P.O. Box 4200 Blair, NE 68009-4200 or you may access the www.eHarlequin.com Web site through January 15, 2002.

Contest sponsored by Torstar Corp., P.O. Box 9042, Buffalo, NY 14269-9042, U.S.A.

PHWDACONT2

# COMING SOON...

AN EXCITING
OPPORTUNITY TO SAVE
ON THE PURCHASE OF
HARLEQUIN AND
SILHOUETTE BOOKS!

**DETAILS TO FOLLOW
IN OCTOBER 2001!**

*YOU WON'T WANT TO MISS IT!*

PHQ401